Only You

THE FITZPATRICKS
BOOK TWO

MELISSA SCHROEDER

COVER ART BY
SCOTT CARPENTER

HARMLESS PUBLISHING

Also by Melissa Schroeder

THE HARMLESS WORLD

The Original Harmless Five

- A Little Harmless Sex
- A Little Harmless Pleasure
- A Little Harmless Obsession
- A Little Harmless Lie
- A Little Harmless Addiction

Rough 'n Ready

- Rough Submission
- Rough Fascination
- Rough Fantasy
- Rough Ride

Harmless Trouble

- Harmless Secrets
- Harmless Revenge
- Harmless Scandals

The Wulf Family

- Faith
- Taboo
- Trust

A Little Harmless Military Romance

- Infatuation
- Possession
- Surrender

Task Force Hawaii

- Seductive Reasoning
- Hostile Desires
- Constant Craving
- Tangled Passions
- Wicked Temptations
- Twisted Emotions-coming 2025

THE CAMOS AND CUPCAKES WORLD

Camos and Cupcakes

- Delicious
- Luscious
- Scrumptious

The Fillmore Siblings

- Hate to Love You
- Love to Hate You

Juniper Springs

- Wild Love
- Crazy Love
- Last Love
- Imperfect Love

- Undeniable
- Unpredictable
- Unexpected
- Tempted

Mafia Sisters

- Stealing Destiny
- Guarding Fable

Faking It

- Faking it with my Billionaire Boss
- Faking it with my Brother's Best Friend
- Faking it with my Frenemy

The Fighting Sullivans

- Falling for the General's Daughter
- Falling for the Girl Next Door
- Falling for my Best Friend
- Falling for my Baby Mama

Also Included

- Kiss my Tinsel
- Dad Bod Rockstar

Texas Temptations

- Conquering India
- Delilah's Downfall

- Primal Instincts

Texas Heat

- Scorched

Spies, Lies, and Alibis

- The Boss

SINGLE TITLES

- A Calculated Seduction
- Chasing Luck
- Going for Eight
- Grace Under Pressure
- Operation Love
- Saving Thea
- Snowbound Seduction
- Sweet Patience
- The Last Detail
- The Seduction of Widow McEwan

One

Declan Fitzpatrick groaned when his phone vibrated on his bedside table. He'd had a long night, thanks to a couple of drunk firefighters. Why any man would fight over a woman who had been playing them both was beyond him. Those assholes not only lost the young woman since she'd hightailed it out of the bar, but the guys were both sporting black eyes. The only thing that saved them from being arrested was that they were both too drunk to do much damage —other than to their pride. He didn't think either of them would ever hear the end of it from their firehouse.

Finally, his phone stopped vibrating. Thank God. He rolled over, snuggled deeper into his bed, and drifted back to sleep. Since he'd closed last night, and his restaurant was closed for his parents' anniversary party, he could roll around in bed as long as he wanted today. He just had to be at the restaurant no later than two.

Just as his mind started to shut down and his body was completely relaxed, his phone vibrated again.

With a groan, he rolled back over and grabbed the phone.

Without looking at who called—because he was sure it was his sister Kaitlin calling about the party—he answered.

"What?"

"Oh, now that's rude," his mother said.

Dammit. "Sorry, Ma."

"No, I'm sorry because I just realized you closed last night. I shouldn't have called this early, but I wanted to make sure you didn't need any help with the party."

He smiled despite the way his head was pounding. Deidre Fitzpatrick was crafty, but he knew her too well. "Let me guess. You tried to help, and Kaitlin wouldn't let you."

There was a pause. He could almost hear her brain moving through her options for attack. Deidre Fitzpatrick had raised six kids, five of them boys, so she had a hard time letting go. She didn't interfere, like his sister's aunt-in-law, Joey Santini, but she always wanted to help. He and his siblings had already told her she couldn't help them. This was their present to their parents, and his mother hated that everyone was doing something for her.

"No."

He chuckled. "Should I call her and ask?"

Another long pause, then a sigh. "Oh, pooh. I just wanted to help."

Declan was a stereotypical Irish American man when it came to his Ma. Worse. His love of cooking had always kept him underfoot in the kitchen. He was probably the closest to her out of his brothers, so he knew her well.

"Did she offer to let you babysit? That will keep you busy."

Kaitlin had recently had the first Fitzpatrick grandbaby.

"No."

"Call her back and tell her you want to watch Little Mike."

"She'll probably tell me that she doesn't need help."

His mother was a helper. Always had been, always would be. He was sure she would still be trying to help in her nineties. Kaitlin had joked that their mother had probably already written down a plan for her wake and funeral.

"Tell her you want to spend time with your grandson on your special day."

"You are my favorite child."

That was a lie because his mother didn't have a favorite child. She loved them all with abandon. All six of them knew they could count on her to be in their corner no matter what.

"And, next week, we could do a baking day."

Fitzpatricks had been in the fire department since the first fire department opened in Baltimore. Declan had been the one to break tradition. He had been the kid who was more interested in how to make the perfect Shepherd's pie rather than how to put out a fire. He tried to carve out one day a month to spend with his mother in the kitchen.

"Oh, now, that sounds like a grand idea. Okay, we'll do that on Wednesday."

That was his regular day off. And, yes, he baked on his day off. It was one of his favorite things to do, and when you ran a bar and grill, you didn't do a lot of baking.

"You got it. We need to plan our Memorial Day cookie drive."

"Of course."

She said nothing else, which was odd. For a librarian, she was always very chatty. He had always thought they would be quiet since they shushed everyone all day, but maybe because she had to be quiet at work, she exploded with chatter when she got home. So, her pause worried him.

"What?"

"I heard Eileen O'Reilly is going to be there."

When his mother said the Baltimore Police Detective's name, his entire body reacted. It was disconcerting that as a man in his thirties, his dick twitched while on the phone with his mother. It had been that way since the moment he'd met her. Eileen had been oblivious of him, not for his lack of trying. The detective always had something on her mind, and it wasn't him.

"Yes. And she has a plus one." Which irritated him, but it wasn't like he had asked her out. Ever.

"Hmm, probably one of her brothers."

"Listen, Ma, I need to get a little more rest before heading to the restaurant."

"Of course. I'll see you tonight."

"Love you."

"Love you, Declan."

He hung up the phone. Of course, he didn't go back to sleep. His mind and body were now wholly focused on the woman he had been infatuated with for nearly six months.

It wasn't something he was used to. He wasn't a womanizer but rarely had trouble closing the deal with women. If they weren't interested, Declan had no problem moving on. His mother had raised him right. But he hadn't even worked up the nerve to ask her out.

It was those eyes. They were somewhere between blue and green. When she showed up at his restaurant, he always ensured she had what she needed. Eileen had a lot of late nights as a homicide detective in Baltimore, and more than one night, she showed up at his place after a long shift. There was something about how she hummed when she ate whatever he put in front of her.

Dammit. Now he was fully aroused.

Knowing that he wouldn't get back to sleep, he slipped out of bed to jump into a cold shower. By the time he was done, he was shivering, but at least he had his need under control.

He grabbed his phone again and decided to check in with his sister. They were the two in charge of the menu for the party.

"Hey, shouldn't you be sleeping?"

"I should, but Ma called. She wanted to complain that you wouldn't let her do anything."

She chuckled. "Yeah, well, she can just stuff it. This is a party for her and Dad. She needs to take a backseat."

"Good luck with that."

Another laugh. A male murmur was in the background, and he knew it was his brother-in-law, Brando Santini.

"Yeah, well, she keeps bugging me about the guest list. I told her we had RSVPs from everyone."

In his head, he told himself not to ask. He had been cautious about how he responded to Eileen around his family. He didn't need any of them getting in his way or causing problems. The Fitzpatricks were very good at causing drama.

"Ma mentioned Eileen was coming."

Silence. He could practically feel his sister's curiosity pulse over the telephone.

"She is. The plus one is her brother, Zane. No. It's Zach. Dang, I can't remember what Wendy told me. I guess it doesn't matter which one since they're twins."

He let out a breath he hadn't realized he was holding.

"Well, since Ma woke me up, I'm getting up. I'll be down at the restaurant around noon."

"I'll see you there."

After they hung up, he stared at the ceiling, his thoughts lingering on the delectable detective. She was no-nonsense, a bit abrupt, and she knew how to handle herself. He'd seen her take care of a few rowdy frat boys one night in his restaurant. She'd scared the shit out of them with whatever she'd said. He smiled at the memory. Then it faded.

This infatuation wasn't something he was used to. This wasn't attraction. It was like a teenage crush. Or obsession, which did not sit well with him.

He had a lot on his plate today and didn't have time to sit on his bed, crushing on a woman who always seemed to have more to do than deal with him.

With that thought, he slipped out of bed and decided to go for a run. That was the only thing he seemed to be able to do these days that got Eileen off his mind.

BY THE TIME his sister and Wendy made it to the restaurant, he had the tables in place. He'd rearranged the floor for the DJ they'd hired and a little room to dance.

"Nice, bro," Kaitlin said as she put a box on the bar. "We were going to help with that."

He gave her a hug. Out of all of them, she looked more like their mother. Her happiness made her glow. Brando made her happy, and he would always be grateful for that. They started off rocky with a surprise pregnancy after one night together. Still, that man knew exactly how to handle his sister.

All six kids had their mother's fair hair, but Kaitlin was more petite like their mother. Their personalities matched, too. She was a helper just like his Ma.

"First of all, it took me all of about thirty minutes. And both of you are doing other things."

"Still," she said as she wandered away. He knew her mind was on about a hundred different things.

Wendy shook her head. "You know, Kaitlin. She wants to help with everything. Just like your mom."

He gave Wendy a hug, just like his sister. Wendy was her best friend and had been an honorary Fitzpatrick for years before Aeden, and she fell in love.

"So, Ma called you too?"

She nodded as she stepped back. "And Aeden."

"You sure you should be up doing this? It's going to be a long day."

She waved his concerns away. "I'm pregnant, not injured."

"Yeah, but I bet you're tired because when Kaitlin was at the end of her second trimester, she was always tired."

Wendy was four months pregnant with a little girl.

"I was off yesterday, and I did nothing but lay around. It was glorious."

"Hey, do we want to get the tables set now?" Kaitlin called out.

Wendy and Declan shared a smile. She was already trying to push them along.

"Yeah, let me get the tablecloths," Declan said. "You wanted the blue ones, right?"

He didn't have an extensive inventory of tablecloths. His bar and grill wasn't the type to do that, but every now and then, he booked the restaurant out. These were for the buffet tables. When he returned, his sister and Wendy were already working on the tables.

"Ma call you again?" Kaitlin asked as she put a flower arrangement on one of the tables.

"No."

"Hmm," was all she said, then, "Did I tell you Eileen is coming?'

"Yes. Yesterday morning, when we talked on the phone." He was still irritated with his attraction and the fact that she would be at the party, but he was excited at the same time.

"Not you," she said.

Declan looked up to find both of them women staring at him. His obsession started affecting his ability to keep his wits about him.

"Oh."

She studied him briefly, then turned back to her best friend. "Anyway, I made sure to text Joey about her. She has that nephew she's trying to set up with everyone."

"What the hell?"

Again, both women looked at him before his sister asked, "You *do* know that Eileen dates, right?"

"Of course, I know that."

He didn't like it, but he knew she did. Or he assumed. Thankfully, he had never had to deal with her bringing a date into his restaurant. Declan understood a woman as stunning and interesting as Eileen would probably get asked out a lot. He just didn't want to think about it."

"He's coming because he and Ma get along so well. He has a bookstore in that little town just west of Warrenton."

"Why would Eileen care about a guy who lives in Virginia?"

He spat the state name like it was poison. It garnered another look from both of the women.

"She's young, gorgeous, and you should see her with kids." She looked at Wendy. "He has a little boy."

"I thought Santinis married for life," Wendy said.

It was true. Most people who knew the Santinis, which seemed to be at least half of the Marine Corps since they all served, knew that once a Santini fell in love, they did not walk away. It was one thing he loved about Brando.

"He's a widower."

Declan wanted to demand that he be uninvited. He didn't need some damned Santini strutting around his restaurant, flaunting his stupid Santini genes in front of Eileen.

Jesus. *What the fuck, Fitzpatrick?* He needed to get his emotions under control, or both his sister and Wendy would pick up on it.

"I need to double-check on the produce for tonight."

Then he rushed out of the room, heading to the kitchen. The staff wouldn't arrive for another couple of hours since the entire restaurant was closed for the party. The room was quiet, and that was what he needed. He had seemed to be losing his control whenever Eileen was mentioned.

He leaned against the counter and did not even look at the produce. He knew, without a doubt, they had enough. Everything had been double and triple-checked.

His phone buzzed in his pocket, and he pulled it out. It was texts from his mother. He shook his head but ended up grinning. She had sent the kid's pics of Little Mike with Big Mike—his father.

His heart warmed as he scrolled through the images. His parents had been involved in their lives as they grew up. Even his father's job as a fireman and later Firehouse Captain hadn't gotten in the way. He had missed a few games here and there, but Mike always knew when one of his kids had something important going on. It might have been his mother making sure he knew, but he went that extra mile and reached out to them. Hell, he had kept up with what was going on with Declan while he was away at culinary school.

He slipped his phone back into his pocket and decided to push his thoughts about Eileen back and concentrate on the party.

"HE IS SO OBVIOUS," Kaitlin said the moment her brother was out of earshot.

"Joey is not trying to set up Brennan. That was mean," Wendy said, but she was smiling when she said it. She carried a box of centerpieces over to one of the tables. After she set it down, she pulled one out.

Kaitlin waved that away, then grabbed two centerpieces. "How many months has he been mooning over her? You would think he didn't know how to handle a woman. He hasn't been on a date in forever."

Wendy frowned. "How do you know that he hasn't been dating?"

"The bros told me. They all find it hilarious. Didn't Aedan say anything about it?"

"No." She already had her phone out and was probably texting Aedan.

Sorry, bro.

"Interesting." And she understood. The truth was that Wendy seemed to have lost her train of thought lately and just blurted things out. She was usually better at keeping secrets, but pregnancy hormones were doing a number on her brain cells. She told Kaitlin she used all her good brain cells at work. She was a nurse in the trauma ward, so that seemed more important than keeping secrets. Hence why Aedan probably didn't tell her.

"Still, you should be nicer to him. Especially after all the work he did for this."

Kaitlin looked around and felt a little guilty. She knew he had not only planned the whole menu but also donated the restaurant and his staff as part of the party. They were getting paid, but it was coming out of Declan's pocket. Whenever one of the siblings tried to pay him for that part of it, he refused. He said he would put it towards the food, liquor, or DJ.

"Okay, I will be nicer, but he needs to get out of his funk."

"True."

"And he has been infatuated with her since she first walked in here. And the fact that she comes here a lot means she likes him too."

"You don't know that."

"This," she said, waving her hands around, "is a fireman bar. She's a cop. They usually go to Houlihan's Bar and Grill, a few streets over. She doesn't."

"Okay, I'll give you that."

"We just need to figure out how to get these two together."

Wendy's eyes widened. "You need to stay out of his business."

Kaitlin said nothing, just nodded, even though she wasn't really agreeing. Wendy should know better because she'd been around the family for a decade. Fitzpatricks believed in family, and by that, she meant meddling was just a way of life for them.

Two

E ileen O'Reilly heard a murmur move through the office, pulling her attention from the report she was working on. Her brother Zach strode through the office. It took him a while to make it to her because he kept getting stopped by her co-workers. The O'Reillys were well known in this precinct since it had been her father's when he was a cop. They were related to a lot of the people in this office either by blood or marriage. The fact that Zach was former FBI and had a lot of contacts only added to the number of people stopping him.

He was dressed in a suit, which wasn't odd for him, even on a Saturday. Since he and his twin Zane had left the FBI, they ran their security firm and charged a pretty penny for their services. Their suits probably cost more than her monthly salary.

"What are you doing here?" she asked after he finally reached her desk.

"Hi, Eileen. How are you?" Zach asked, sarcasm dripping from every word.

She rolled her eyes. Both of her brothers gave her crap for

being too abrupt. She didn't understand why people had to do small talk—not with family.

"Sorry, I forgot how sensitive you are. How are you today?"

He sighed and sat down in the chair next to her desk. "Irritated."

Inwardly, she groaned. Out of the three siblings, Zach was the most emotional. Or, as Zane called him: ALOW—a lot of work. If he was in the mood to vent, there was no getting around it. She had a pile of work to get done before running home to prepare for an anniversary party for the Fitzpatricks.

Then it hit her. She narrowed her eyes as she studied him. "No, you promised to go with me."

He couldn't back out on her this late in the game. She needed him there. He and Zane were her buffer against...Eileen didn't want to even think his name. And she knew that Zane was in DC on a case. Before he could respond to her comment, they were interrupted.

"Hey, Zach," a voice said behind her, and she managed not to roll her eyes, but it was close. She knew that voice, unfortunately. Working in the same precinct as your ex was difficult, but she didn't have a choice. "What are you doing here?"

Zach kept eye contact with her for a long moment before looking up at Bryan Comstock. "Talking with my sister, *Bryan*."

Zach had never liked her ex. Actually, neither of her brothers liked him. They tended to leave her alone about who she dated, but Bryan...they both had a distaste for him from the moment they'd met him. Mainly because they deemed him lazy and arrogant, which Eileen refused to admit at the time. Now, she had to deal with him almost daily.

It might be that he was a legacy like her. Bryan and Eileen came from a long line of cops, but Bryan always seemed to think he deserved more. Hell, half the station house were legacies. Most of them had something to prove, and they worked twice as hard. Bryan was the one who expected something because of his last name, and he rarely had a good reputation, no matter what department he worked. The only solace she had was that she'd beat him out at the academy on every level, which was why they didn't last. She also made detective a whole year ahead of him and was now working in homicide. He had just made detective and was working in Vice.

Knowing she had no choice, she turned and looked at him. He was dressed down for the day in jeans and a Ravens sweatshirt. His hair was short, cut meticulously, and probably by someone who charged more than she would pay. He had chocolate brown eyes that had once been her downfall. She now understood he could fake empathy.

When she said nothing, her brother decided to poke Bryan. "I guess we could ask the same thing, Bryan. You're not dressed for work."

"I forgot my gym bag here yesterday. Didn't want it to be ripe by Monday. Plus, I had to get out to pick up some flowers for my date tonight."

Neither Zach nor Eileen said anything to that. With Bryan, it was better to just cut him off. If not, you were going to be stuck talking to him forever.

"Okay, well, I'll see you later."

When he finally left, she released a breath. Eileen hadn't realized how the muscles in her back had tensed during the very short interaction.

"I still have no idea why you dated him."

She looked at him. "I was young and stupidly thought he accepted my career choice."

"He didn't?"

"He did, but he got mad every time I did better than him. He wanted to be the big, bad detective, and he told me he would make it before I would."

Zach's mouth twitched. "Oh, that's fantastic."

"Now, back to the point, you were being a rat bastard."

He rolled his eyes. "I have to head out of town. It can't be helped. But I have a replacement."

Maybe she could just say something came up at work, and she couldn't make the party. There would be so many people there that she wouldn't be missed. The Fitzpatricks definitely understood that work could get in the way of your personal life. Their family had served in the fire department about as long as hers had for Baltimore PD.

Well, except Declan, who owned a restaurant.

Dammit. She just thought his name, and now she would lose time thinking about him. Because that always happened when a stray thought about the sexy chef danced through her head. There was so much to like about him, and she had been trying to resist his magnetic pull for months. Not that he seemed all that interested, but she couldn't get her hormones to understand. She was having dreams about him, like some lovelorn teen. She couldn't remember ever being this infatuated with a man.

"Don't. You know you want to be there. But lucky for you, Rowan is in town."

Before she could respond to that, she heard their cousin's voice. "Eileen!"

She shot her brother a dirty look before turning towards

their cousin. He was making his way through the bullpen, but he didn't stop to talk to anyone. He was related to them, just like she and Zach, but he was different, like in a unicorn kind of way different.

He was in the Navy, and while he wasn't supposed to tell anyone, he was a SEAL. She wasn't sure which team he was on, but he was stationed in California. That military training made him ignore everything but his target, and that was apparently her.

Before she could say anything, he plucked her out of her chair and hugged her. As always, he smelled like the beach. All saltwater and freshness. From age five, he always wanted to be in the water. And while she wasn't happy about what her brother was trying to pull, she had missed Rowan.

"Put me down, you idiot."

He laughed and did as she ordered. "You know we can tell you love us because you call us names."

That was true. She was exceedingly polite to people she didn't like.

"Why didn't you tell us you were returning for a visit?"

"Wanted to surprise my Ma and Da. I hear we get to go to Fitzpatrick's tonight."

She sighed. "I guess you are my plus one now?" His smile widened into a grin. Eileen looked at her brother. "I can go on my own."

"Noooo, Eileen! I know the Santinis. Marco and I went through training together."

Kaitlin Fitzpatrick-Santini's in-laws were legendary in the Marines and Navy. Everyone knew the family, but she understood the reference. He couldn't say out loud that they went to SEAL training together, not in the open. But she did know that

MELISSA SCHROEDER

the bonds formed during SEAL training lasted decades for some of them. Marco lived in Hawaii, so she assumed he must still be on teams.

"Fine, but no messing around with the women in that family. I do not need to have that Joey Santini after me, and she will come after me if you break hearts."

"I will be a true gentleman."

"That will be a first."

"So it's fixed. He can be your date, and I can go do my thing. Win. Win." Zach smiled like he had solved some great mystery.

"You needed a date? You could have asked me."

Ugh, there was Bryan again. She turned to look at her ex, who was indeed holding a gym bag.

"She doesn't need you," Zach said. It was out of character for him to be so blunt, but he was always like that with Bryan. "Besides, didn't you just say you had a date?"

Her golden retriever of a cousin looked between the two of them, assessing the situation, and his smile faded. A steely look entered his eyes, and she knew that was his SEAL face, as he called it. She did not need a pissing contest right by her desk. It was hard enough being one of the few women in homicide.

"It's more of a family thing, Bryan," Eileen said.

"Oh, okay. See ya later."

Once he was out of earshot, Rowan said, "What an asshole."

"You don't know him."

Although, she didn't know why she was getting defensive. She didn't like Bryan. Worse, she didn't trust him. He wasn't a bad guy, but he definitely had a chip on his shoulder and

18

wanted more than anything to be in homicide. He would take anyone out if he thought it would get him a spot.

"Your brother thinks he's an asshole, so I do too. Also, who says that to an ex? Asshole. And weird. Really weird."

"I thought you didn't have much to do with him," her brother said.

She sighed. "Hard to avoid all the time since we're in the same precinct." She felt like a broken record. Both her brothers asked the question a lot. "Besides, don't you have to be somewhere?"

"Yeah. Have fun tonight, half-pint."

"Shut it."

He laughed, and her heart danced. As much as her brothers irritated her, she loved them twice as much. Even when they called her by her dreaded nickname.

"I'll pick you up at your place. What's the dress code?"

"Suit, and I'll drive."

He made a face. "Suit? Really?"

"Hey, you want to be seen with me, you will wear dress pants and not jeans."

"Fine. C'ya, cuz."

Once they finally left her alone, she got back into her paperwork. She was still adjusting to life without her first partner as a detective. He deserved his retirement.

It didn't take long for her to finish the paperwork and start digging into the cold case of Norma Wilson.

Norma Wilson had been her mother's teacher, not too many years older than her, and had been murdered. Her body had been left in an alley, and it had taken Baltimore PD a few days to figure out who she was. In 1987, the authorities didn't have the type of technology they now have.

So young, blond, pretty...but the scene had left little to the imagination. Stripped of every possession, even her clothes, she had been left off Fleet Street. Eileen had promised her mother she would look into the case, but there had been little to look into. There was some DNA, but once they could enter it in the system, nothing popped.

Still, she wanted to be honest with her mother. Looking into the case and maybe talking it over with a few cops. And truthfully, Eileen knew the case already. When she had joined the academy, she had talked about it all the time. But it had been years since she had really looked into it again. So, hopefully, all of her training and experience would help.

The one thing that always stood out to her was the knife in the woman's chest. It was custom-made. Expensive. Hard to believe that they couldn't seem to figure out where it had come from. With her remaining time, she decided to search for any references to a knife like the one used, and maybe she could find out where it was sold.

HER DOORBELL RANG RIGHT on time. Of course, Rowan had driven her crazy with multiple texts about what he should wear. Then came the pictures. She didn't care what tie he wore, but apparently, he did. He was military, which meant if you weren't early, you were late. At least, that's what he'd said to her earlier.

She opened the door and smiled at her cousin.

"You do clean up nice, Rowan."

And he did. Unlike her side of the family, Rowan had light

hair and dark eyes. He looked like his mother, while his sister looked like her father, like the other O'Reillys.

"I could say the same thing about you. Showing a lot of leg. And those heels...who are you trying to impress?"

"First," she said, turning away to grab her wrap and purse. "I dress for myself. Second, you sound like a sexist jerk who thinks the only thing women think about are men."

"I don't think that," he said, frowning at her as she set her alarm and locked her door.

"You don't?"

"No. I think lesbians think about women."

She sighed. "Rowan. That's inappropriate." She knew he wasn't a sexist; it was just that sometimes he said things before he could think them through.

"I mean, I think about women a lot. Like, look at this." He waved his hands down his outfit. "I did this because I want to impress women."

"You dressed like that because I threatened you."

"Well, that too, but I would have done it anyway. Also, Mrs. Santini will be there. She kind of scares me."

She laughed. Joey Santini *was* kind of scary, but in a good way. The woman loved her family, and if she thought you should be part of it, she would do everything she could to get you there. "Join the club. Come on, cuz, we're running late."

He offered her his arm, and she took it. She did love Rowan. He was a total golden retriever kind of guy, but since he'd entered the military and then got on teams, he had been different. There was a bit of an edge to him. He'd also put on about twenty pounds of pure muscle. Still, the two of them had grown up together. Only three months separated them in age.

They went to school together and often hung out all through high school. And she missed him a lot.

Once they were on their way, Rowan decided to play interrogator.

"Is there a reason you didn't want to go alone? Because, while I'm thrilled to be going, you're not the kind of person who has to have a plus one."

She took a right turn off her street. She actually didn't live that far from where Declan's establishment was. "I just didn't want to go alone."

"Nope, not buying it. I think you needed one of two things."

She slanted him a look. "What would those be?"

"One, you want a wingman, and let me tell you, I am an excellent wingman."

He would be. She was pretty sure his dimples and personality put a lot of women at ease.

"And the second one?"

"You need a buffer. There's someone there you're trying to resist. It's not someone bothering you because you would kick them in the nuts." He chuckled. "Ritchie Manso learned that the hard way."

"That creep deserved it."

"He did. But you didn't go to your brothers or any of your multitude of male cousins. Instead, you kneed him so hard, I don't think that bastard will ever have kids."

She smiled at the memory. "Ritchie has been married twice and has six kids."

"What? Why? How?"

"Use your words, Rowan."

"Why would anyone marry him?"

She shrugged. "Not sure."

"Oh, wait, there is a third option."

"What would that be?"

"You're trying to make him jealous."

She blinked, then started laughing.

"What?"

"Dude, I was taking my brother first, and you're my cousin. If I wanted to make a guy jealous, which is so not me, I could get someone from work to go with me. I definitely don't want to go all inbreeder on a guy. The guys interested in that would not be my cup of tea."

There was a beat of silence, then he cracked up. "Okay, I didn't think that last one out. I'm betting on the second option."

She looked away and noticed the light had turned green.

"Oh, yeah, that's it."

"What?"

"You always avoid eye contact when you lie or are avoiding the truth. It is one of your big tells."

It was? And yes, people forgot to be on guard around Rowan because of those dimples and his sparkly eyes. Even his cousin.

"Listen, it's not so much of avoiding temptation as avoiding making a fool of myself. I'm not the guy's type because I've seen them."

"Well, he sounds like an asshole. Let me beat him up."

She smiled. "I've missed you."

"I've missed you too. You need to come to see me in Cali. You would love it there."

"No. It sounds too sunny and optimistic. I need cold weather and dreariness a few months out of the year."

He laughed as she pulled into the parking garage down the street from Fitzpatrick's. Once she parked, Eileen checked her phone one last time.

"What?"

"I'm on call this weekend. Just want to make sure I didn't miss anything."

They both slipped out of the car. She locked it, then joined him at the back. He offered his arm once again.

"Shall we?"

Again, she smiled because she was happy that he was home and in one piece for now.

"We shall."

Three

"You did a good job, Declan," his mother said. He looked at his mom. Deidre was fiercely loyal, independent, and hard-headed. He never had to question her love for him, and when he chose culinary school over the firehouse, she was the first one he told.

"I didn't do all of it. Kaitlin organized everything."

"And you helped. I know all of you boys did, but you the most. The others are not good with organizing, not like you and Kaitlin."

"Dad seems to be having a great time."

They both watched his father as he talked to a group of his parents' friends.

The whirlwind that was Conrad Santini came barreling through, followed by Joey Santini. She was laughing as she watched him run to his father. He watched as the man picked him up. That connection...it left him envious. He had never thought wanting a child would hit him, but when Kait had little Mike, and now with Wendy pregnant with a girl, he was.

This need started when Kait had Mike right after Wendy returned from her work abroad.

He frowned. He'd been thinking of that more and more, but it had more to do with Eileen. She had him thinking of things like that, but he hadn't even gotten a kiss from her.

The door opened as if the gods controlled fate, and she stepped inside. Jesus, his heart was pounding, but the way she was dressed...

Declan was used to seeing her in her pantsuits—which he loved. But this...this made his head spin and left his palms sweaty. Eileen wasn't a curvy woman. She was more athletic, with long, lean muscles and an ass he had fantasized about a little too much. The dress she wore... clung to her, making the most of all of her assets. Everything around him faded as he watched her laugh at something and look back at someone who was definitely not her brother. He shot a dirty look at his sister. Kaitlin shrugged.

Without taking his gaze off her, Declan made his way over to her and the jerk she brought with her to *his* parents' party. His mom had already cornered Eileen before she could even talk to anyone. The stupid guy with her had his mother laughing before Declan made it to the trio. He was tall and fit. Probably not a cop, but there was something about him. The other man reminded him of Kaitlin's husband, Brando, who was a Marine but was teaching at the University of Maryland right now.

By the time he arrived, he had worked himself into a real temper.

"I'm so glad you could both make it. Sorry about Zane."

Eileen smiled at his mother and opened her mouth to answer when she made eye contact with Declan over his mother's shoulder.

His mother turned around. "Oh, Declan. Eileen made it!"

Yeah, and she brought some jerk-face idiot who probably thought he had a chance with Eileen.

"I see," was all he said.

One eyebrow lifted as Eileen studied him.

"I thought Zane was going to be with you tonight."

His mother shot him a weird look. Declan knew his comment sounded like an accusation.

"I was just explaining to your mother that he had something come up at work. They had an issue with a client."

He nodded, and then his gaze turned to her date. He hated him on sight. The guy's smile widened as he stuck out his hand.

"Rowan O'Reilly, Eileen's favorite cousin."

The relief coursing through his blood left him dizzy. He took the man's hand and studied him. There were similarities around the eyes, and they had the same face shape. But he was fairer than Eileen, with light brown hair and light blue eyes.

"That's not true. Mary Ellen is my favorite cousin." Eileen's voice was amused.

"Then I'm your favorite male cousin."

"Okay. I will give you that."

"Nice to meet you. Is this your first time to Fitzpatrick's?"

He shook his head. "But it has been a while. I'm stationed in California."

Stationed. He had pegged him as military, and he had been right.

"Rowan is in the Navy," his mother said. "And he knows—"

"O'Reilly!"

He turned to see Brando hurrying over with little Mike in his arms.

"Santini, good to see you," he said, giving the man a side hug and then looking down at the baby. "A mini Santini."

"Come on over. Aunt Joey would love to see you, I'm sure."

"Do you mind?" he asked Eileen.

"You invited yourself, so go do what you want to."

"Thanks, cuz," he said, giving her a kiss on her cheek.

"Oh, I need to find your father so he can't sneak away when the dancing starts."

Then, he was alone with Eileen.

"So, your cousin?"

"Yeah. He trained with Marco Santini so when my turncoat brother told me he had something come up, he foisted the golden retriever on me."

He glanced at her cousin, who was now holding little Mike and talking to Joey, and then Declan turned back to Eileen.

"You call a guy who can probably kill someone with two fingers a golden retriever."

She smiled, and her eyes sparkled. Fuck, she was beautiful.

"So maybe a golden/pit-bull mix."

"You look nice."

She tilted her head and studied him for a second. "Do I normally not look nice?"

She had done something with her eyes that made them look more blue than green tonight, and she was wearing dangling earrings. She usually wore studs.

"No, you always look nice. You just look different."

He opened his mouth to say something else, but they were interrupted by his sister and Wendy.

"Eileen, I'm so happy you could make it," Kaitlin said. She hugged Kaitlin, then Wendy.

28

"Thank you for the invite. Nice to get out on a Saturday night."

"Come on over, I need you to meet someone."

His sister was already tugging her away. "I guess I'll catch you later."

He watched as she went with his sister and Wendy. She towered over them both, and that's when he looked down at her legs. Jesus, she was wearing thigh-high boots with heels. She was trying to kill him.

"So, Eileen brought a date," Emmett said, stepping beside him.

"He looks like military, huh? Not a cop." This came from Seamus, another idiot brother. "What will you do when she gets married and moves away? Gonna stalk her on her social media still?"

Fuck, he didn't need to deal with them tonight. "That's her cousin, and he lives in California, which probably frowns on first cousins marrying." And he didn't stalk her on social media because she had none.

"Hmm, but you wanted to kick his ass. That was easy to see," Emmett says.

If he responded, it would end up in a fight. He would not punch either of his brothers at his parents' anniversary party.

So, pushing aside his anger, he said, "Get bent."

Then headed off to check things in the kitchen. He wanted to ensure he was back out there before the dancing started because he was determined to get Eileen in his arms.

TWO HOURS INTO THE PARTY, Eileen was stuffed. She hadn't meant to eat like she'd been stuck on a desert island for three years, but when it was Declan's recipes, she couldn't resist.

"Your chef wanted to beat me up," Rowan said.

"He's not mine."

He snorted. "Believe me, cuz, that guy wants you to be his. He wanted to pull off my arms and beat me with them."

She rolled her eyes.

"He's never been in the military?"

She shook her head. "Nope. Went to culinary school when he was eighteen."

"Weird because with his build and awareness...he makes me think of the military."

"Yeah," she said. She knew what Rowan meant. Declan was the biggest of all his brothers, but there was grace in how he moved. She watched as he threw back his head and laughed. God, he was so damned sexy.

"No calls?"

She tore her gaze from her crush. "No, thank God. I hope it holds out for the night."

"So no one was killed tonight."

"No. It means they have enough personnel to handle it."

She tried to keep her attention off Declan but found her gaze wandering back to the chef. He was holding the little Santini boy. In all her thirty-two years, she had never really thought about things like kids. She was sure she did as a young girl, but when she zeroed in on being a cop, she left those thoughts behind. She never thought she would be one of those women who could juggle a career and marriage with kids. But seeing Declan with that little boy made her...yearn. Jesus, she had never used that word associated with a man and a happily-ever-after.

"What's with that guy Bryan? I mean, you guys dated like five years ago."

Thankful that her cousin pulled her out of her fugue, she shrugged.

"From what I heard, he and his girlfriend just broke up."

"And what? He decided to try and get the woman back that stomped on his heart."

She turned to face her cousin. "I did not stomp on his heart. It was his ego."

That was all it was. He'd never truly loved her. She suspected that Bryan was a sociopath who would never love the woman he was with if she wasn't one hundred percent committed to him. As in, no friends, no career, only Bryan. Why he thought she would be the one for him, she had no idea.

"He looked like a puppy dog looking at you today."

"He did not. Besides, if he was kissing up to me, it was to help his career."

"Another ego killer. You graduated from the academy together, didn't you?"

She nodded. Rowan opened his mouth to ask another annoying question, and she was thankful that a shout from one of the Santinis pulled his attention away.

"Be right back."

"Don't rush," she said with a laugh. She really loved her cousin. He annoyed her because he had always been like that. Always asking questions, his mind bouncing from one subject to the other. But it was good to see him.

"Your cousin seems to know the Santinis well," a deep voice

whispered in her ear. She fought the shiver that worked down her spine.

How Declan could sneak up behind her, she had no idea. He was a big man, but he always seemed to move around, making no sound.

She glanced at him. "He trained with Marco, Joey's son who lives in Hawaii."

"Hmm, so that makes him a SEAL."

She shrugged and sipped her water.

"Not drinking, detective?"

She shook her head. "I'm on call."

He nodded. "I didn't get to tell you just how nice you look tonight."

She would not preen, but damn, it was hard. He looked at her as if she were the only person in the room. She couldn't remember a man ever looking at her like that.

"Thank you."

A slow song started, and she glanced at the makeshift dance floor that Declan had set up. Her gaze was caught on Wendy and Aeden. Those two were so close so in tune with each other. When she had first met the two of them, it struck her how they seemed to understand each other so well.

All of a sudden, Declan grabbed her glass.

"Hey!"

He took her hand and dragged her to the dance floor, setting the glass on a table as she stumbled behind him.

"Declan, stop."

He turned around and frowned at her. Rude.

"What are you doing?"

"You want to dance."

She did, and specifically with him.

"You know you need to ask a girl to dance before you drag her out to the floor, right?"

"Fine. Want to dance?"

She wanted to laugh. He was so put out by her, making him not a Neanderthal. It was odd because she had seen him with women. He was all charm and smiles. Now, he was frowning at her and growling. What did it say about her that she found this sexier than his charming side?

"Cuz, you need backup?" Rowan asked.

Without breaking eye contact with Declan, she shook he head. "No. I'm waiting for Declan to ask me to dance."

He huffed, actually huffed, then finally asked. "Will you dance with me?"

She smiled at him, and he blinked. It was like he was stunned by it. Did she not smile that much?

"Yes."

Then he took her hand again and pulled her to the dance floor.

The moment he took her into his arms, she felt the world shift, and everything settled. He smelled like sandalwood and home. God, he was a furnace.

"You are not always going to get your way."

She looked up at him. "I rarely do."

That much was true. Every step in her life had been hard fought. Being an O'Reilly helped all of her male cousins in the department. For her, it didn't. Women were still not accepted as cops, even by family.

He pulled her tighter against him. She could feel his galloping heart, and she sighed. The guy was driving her insane, but at least he was being driven in the same direction to the asylum.

"What am I going to do about you?"

He growled the question in her ear, and this time, she couldn't fight the shiver that rolled through her body. Before she could answer him—with exactly what she wanted done to her—she felt her phone vibrate.

Sighing, she stopped dancing.

"What?"

She pulled out her phone, and irritation moved through her when she saw the number.

"Work." She walked away and clicked on her phone. "O'Reilly."

"Hey, Eileen. It's Sammy." Another cousin.

"What do you have?"

"Young woman, not too far from where you are. You're at Fitzpatrick's, right?"

"Yeah. Text me the location. Does Eddie know?"

"Yep."

She hung up and noticed that Declan was still standing there watching her. "Gotta go."

"Of course."

She noticed that his parents were still dancing. "Tell your parents I'm sorry."

"Don't worry. One thing we understand is duty."

"Got your wrap," Rowan said. Another big man who could sneak up on her.

She took it and thanked him. Then she turned to face Declan. "Thank you for the dance."

"We didn't finish."

The way his voice tumbled over those syllables had her heart pounding and her nipples hard. Ugh, how could he do that to her?

"We will finish it."

It sounded like a promise.

She cocked her head to the side, studying him. "I almost believe that."

Then she hurried away.

DECLAN WATCHED Eileen leave his restaurant, her cousin going with her.

"Damn, bro, never thought you would run off the detective," Connal said beside him.

"Well, you do know how charming he is." That came from Emmett.

His brothers were annoying. He was frustrated and didn't want to deal with them. Or anyone. He wanted Eileen back so they could finish that dance.

Declan said nothing as he walked to the bar where one of his other brothers sat.

"What's up?" Seamus asked.

"He ran off his crush," Emmett said.

It took all of his power not to smack his brother. He would not make a scene at his parents' anniversary party.

"Stop messing with him."

Declan gave Seamus a grateful look. "Thanks."

"Just because Declan has lost his mojo with women is nothing to mock."

His fingers turned white as he held onto the edge of the bar. Being one of six siblings, five of them being brothers, they settled their disagreements with physical fights. At least, growing up, they did. Now, it only happened every now and then.

"Declan, come talk to Joey. She's talking about food, and I know the two of you would love to exchange thoughts on her upcoming family reunion."

He glanced over his shoulder at his sister—the best of them. She never physically fought them, but she did intervene from time to time.

"Sure."

He walked with her over to the Santinis' table. "Thanks."

"You're welcome, with a caveat."

He stopped a few feet away from the table and waited. There was never any way to rush Kaitlin.

"You like her."

He nodded, although *like* wasn't actually a big enough word for what he felt. Declan wasn't sure exactly how to describe the feelings he had for her.

"You need to ask her out. Brando and I had crushes on each other in college, and we waited. Thankfully, not too late, but I still mourn all our years apart. Don't waste time, bro."

He sighed and nodded his head.

"Now, get ready because my aunt-in-law wants to talk food, and she's Italian. This will take a bit," she said with a laugh.

Declan nodded and continued to follow her to the table. He definitely needed to do something about Eileen, but tonight was about family which now included the Santinis.

EILEEN PARKED her car on Fleet Street.

"Can I come with you?" Rowan asked.

She rolled her eyes. She'd already said no. "You're a civilian."

"Fine."

The sigh of frustration clogged her throat. She loved her cousin, but she wasn't like a lot of their family. She was a woman in homicide, where they didn't have many women. She couldn't do anything wrong, or she would get demoted or fired.

"It will only take a second to find out what's going on, then I can drop you off."

Without waiting for an answer, she slipped from the car. The street had been blocked off with tape and police cars. Even though she knew one of the uniforms, she flashed her badge.

"Eileen, how's everything?" her cousin Freddy asked. Then he took in her outfit. "Damn, you were on a date."

She snorted. "Hardly. Family anniversary party for some friends. Rowan was my date."

"What the hell? Didn't he want to see me?"

"He's in the car, but before you go, do you know anything?"

A lot of people looked down on uniforms like they all didn't start out that way. Eileen knew better than that.

"Young woman, that's all I know. It was apparently pretty brutal based on the reaction of some of the cops."

She nodded and ducked under the tape. As she walked down the street to the alley where they'd found the body, she nodded to people she knew and almost blinked when the lights came on.

She stepped up beside her partner, Eddie Francisco.

"Well, look at you," he said, smirking.

"Yeah. I'm a hottie. What do we have?"

His smile faded. "Young woman. No idea, but she looks to be in her mid to late twenties."

37

"So, she was robbed? Could this be a mugging gone wrong?"

"Not this. If it started that way, it went way overboard."

She nodded as she put booties on her shoes.

"It's an alley, Eileen."

"Doesn't matter. When your brother used to hunt killers with the FBI, you learn a few things they don't show on TV."

That brought his smile back, albeit not as bright.

She made her way into the alley. The stench of rotting veggies, urine, and, yes, even vomit filled her senses. The idea that someone spent their last moments here made her sad. No one deserved to die in a place like this.

A photographer took pics, and the ME was already on site.

Sharlene Anderson glanced at her. She and the tall African American woman had known each other for a while. They had grown up on the same street. "O'Reilly. Nice dress."

"Thanks. Eddie said that she's in her mid-twenties?"

"Yeah, if that."

Eileen stepped closer and felt her entire world shift. Oh, hell. She had seen something like this scene before. A woman in an alley, young, stripped of every possession and left in a dank alley. The stabbing in her chest... was the same also.

That cold case she had been studying earlier today might have just boiled over.

Four

W hat the actual—

"Eileen?"

She glanced at Sharlene. Even wearing heels, she felt tiny compared to the African American ME. She was over five nine, with sharp dark brown eyes that rarely missed anything. Even standing at a crime scene as bloody as this one, Sharlene looked stunning.

"I might be wrong."

Sharlene let her eyebrow rise up. "You're rarely wrong, and when you are, it's so tiny no one notices."

Eileen wished that was true. What she told her cousin was true. Being an O'Reilly was good, but it put a spotlight on her. Being one of the few women to make it to detective so fast and in homicide no less made her a target. Every asshole in the department who thought they should have been chosen made her life hell. Not outwardly. Just enough to slow down her investigations. But she knew Sharlene had dealt with her share of misogyny.

"This looks just like the Norma Wilson case."

Sharlene pursed her lips. "When was that? I don't think I worked on that case."

"Probably because it happened in 1987."

Her eyes widened as she looked down at the woman. "Did they ever catch the guy?"

Eileen shook her head.

"So...are you thinking this would be the same murderer?"

"God, no. The profile on the guy said he would have been white, in his mid-thirties to late forties. That would make it impossible. Even if he were in his twenties..."

"Not impossible, but definitely improbable."

She nodded. "It's odd to go this long between killings for someone like this." She might not have been FBI like her brothers, but they had taught her a lot. This much rage was hard to contain. The victim might have been stabbed once in the heart, but the bruising and swelling around the face told of the bastard's rage. Plus, stabbing someone in the chest was not an easy feat.

"Does she look like the woman?"

She had the same athletic build, slight curves. There was something familiar about the woman, but it was hard to tell with her face swollen.

"Yeah, except for the dark hair. That's different."

"Hmm. Well, hopefully, I can find out who she is fast."

"How long has she been here?"

"Less than two hours. I hear they have the person who found her in the back of one of the cars."

"Gotcha."

She made her way back out of the alley, trying to hide the

anxiety coursing through her. Eileen was usually good at controlling her nerves. It went with being a cop and, especially, a female cop.

"Does Sharlene have a TOD?" Eddie asked.

"Within the last two hours."

He blew out a breath. "Damn."

"Have you taken the witness statement?"

"Yeah. He was on his way home from work. Chad Baker," he said, signaling with his head.

"Thoughts?"

"Could have done it, but he has no blood on him. Also, I already checked with the restaurant where he works. He only left about ten minutes before he called 911. With her being murdered in the last two hours..."

"Highly unlikely. Although, I guess we'll have to double-check his alibi."

Her partner nodded. "You might want to check him out before we turn him loose."

She walked over and found the man sitting in the back of a squad car. The door was open. He was holding his head in his hands.

"Sir?"

He looked up at her, his gaze a little unfocused. She had seen it before, way too many times. People knew about murders and spent their days and nights watching all kinds of true crime. It was different when you were part of it. Light blue eyes, dirty blond hair, and a slight build. She would put him in his early to mid-twenties.

"Mr. Baker, I was told you found the body?"

He swallowed and nodded. "I was walking down the street

to catch the bus and saw her feet on the other side of the dumpster. I know there are a lot of people who drink too much down here. Working at the bar, I see it all the time."

She nodded. "How did you know it was a woman?"

He shrugged. "Little feet, so I assumed."

The woman was small in stature.

His head was in his hands again. "I thought maybe it was just a mannequin."

Ninety-nine percent of the time, it wasn't a mannequin.

"Okay, Mr. Baker, we will probably have more questions, but I'll have one of the officers take you home."

His head rose. "I can get home on my own."

"I know you can, but sometimes, people in your situation can have delayed responses. Do you live alone?"

He shook his head. "I live with my boyfriend."

"And he's home tonight?"

He nodded.

"Good. Sit tight, and we'll get you home safely."

She did not need this man going into shock on the way home. Watching murder on TV was a lot easier than being up close and personal with it in real life.

After sending one of the officers back to the man, Eileen returned to her partner.

"Yeah, the guy looks like he's going into shock."

He nodded. "Sorry to ruin your night."

She smiled at him. "And yours, too."

"Naw, Avery is teething."

"Oh, so you were happy to abandon your wife."

He snorted. "You've never had a teething kid. I promise you; you would do the same thing."

"Okay, well, I'm gonna drop my degenerate cousin off and change. Should take me about thirty minutes."

He nodded. "Crime scene people are almost done."

When she returned to her car, Rowan was sitting on the hood. Somehow, he'd found a bag of chips. Seriously, where the hell did he get that? He was always eating, probably because of his training. She was sure SEALs ate an insane number of calories.

"Get off before I shoot you."

He licked his fingers. Ugh.

"You can't do that."

"Yes, I can."

He made a face and slid off the hood.

"Did you want to crash at my place? Or did you want me to drop you back at Fitzpatrick's?"

"Naw. I'll be up at O-dark thirty. Are you going back?"

She stopped at a light and slanted him a look. "I just got a body. I have a case to work."

He nodded. "I just thought you would go back to see your boyfriend."

She frowned. "I don't have a boyfriend."

"Declan's not your boyfriend? He sure does act like it. He watched you all night."

Something fluttered in her belly. Stupid butterflies. She was thirty-two years old. She didn't get all giggly over men. Not anymore. She'd learned her lesson. Men didn't like a woman who had other interests, especially when those interests included dead bodies.

"You're imagining things."

"Am not."

"That was mature."

"More mature than pretending that some dude wasn't making goo-goo eyes at you all night."

"He wasn't doing that, and I don't think you can call yourself mature if you use the term *goo-goo* eyes."

"Why don't you ask him out?"

"Why are you being so nosey about my love life?" Or lack thereof. She hadn't been out on a date in months, and those few she'd had in the last year had been...disappointing.

"Answering a question with a question. Dude, you want to date him, but...?"

"Listen, when men find out I'm a cop, they fit into one of two categories. They are repulsed by it because it *is* a guy job."

"That group sounds like a bunch of a-holes."

She snorted as she pulled into her driveway.

"And the second?"

She sighed. "Those dudes are turned on by it."

"And you don't want to date them?"

She glanced over at Rowan to find him frowning at her.

"It's a fetish with them. Like the badge bunnies." She'd always hated that term, but she knew that there were both women and men who wanted to date cops just because they were cops. And if you both understood the situation, she had no problem with it. As a woman in a male-dominated career, she knew she didn't want to deal with that.

"Ugh, okay, but Declan seems like a nice guy."

"Nice guys, don't want to date a woman who is going to spend her Saturday night and Sunday morning working on a murder."

He looked like he wanted to say more, but she didn't have

time. "Listen, we can talk about my non-existent love life later. I have work I have to do, and I know you understand that."

IT WASN'T until eight the following day that they finally had an ID on their victim. Both she and Eddie had gone home to grab an hour or two of sleep. They knew there was a good chance that their captain would be on their asses to get this one solved and fast.

"Irene Adams," Robby said.

She looked over at him.

"That's her name. Sent the info to your phone."

She sighed as she picked up the phone. The moment she saw the ID photo, her breath backed up in her lungs.

"I know her."

"Yeah?"

She nodded as she went through the info they had found on her.

Irene Adams was only twenty-five and had recently moved to Baltimore from Richmond, Virginia. She lived alone.

"She worked at Fitzpatrick's."

And that's how badly her face had been beaten last night. She had looked familiar, but Eileen hadn't been able to place where she knew her from. Again, that was a lot of rage.

Her parents still lived in Richmond, and Eddie offered to do the notification. Even over the phone, it was one of the worst things about this job. As a cop, you will play a starring role in the worst day of people's lives.

Eddie sighed as he set his phone down. "They'll be up here

tonight to identify her. They're in Virginia Beach for their anniversary."

"Damn." And now, every year, they would remember the death of their daughter.

Her phone buzzed, and she looked at it. "Oh, okay, we have some info on an ex. She filed a restraining order against him six months before leaving Richmond."

Eddie's eyebrows shot up. "She filed, then she moved away? That sounds like a lead."

Eileen nodded. "Yeah, the asshole started stalking her after she broke up with him. Then, he escalated and..." her voice drifted off as she read on.

"And?"

"He broke into her house, smacked her around, and threatened her with a knife."

Eddie whistled. "I would say that is a lead."

"Name's Brantley Brown."

"Jesus, who would do that to a kid?"

She looked up at him. "You wanted to name your kid Sam. With the last name of Francisco."

"That's classy. Besides Marguerite said no. She rules the house."

"Hey, guys."

She cringed the moment she heard Bryan's voice. Why the hell was he hanging around the place on a Sunday morning?

"Heard you caught the murder case."

She nodded. "Yep."

"Should we head over to Fitzpatrick's?" Eddie asked loudly. He didn't like Bryan. Now that she thought about it, not many people liked him since they had both started at the department. He had his group of bro dudes, those guys who still acted like they were twenty-two years old while in their thirties and forties. They drank beer, made condescending comments about women, and were gross. They all seemed to think they should get preferential treatment. All of them were legacies, just like her, but she worked twice as hard to prove herself. Those idiots were lazy, and many would probably never move up—unless a family member got them a leg up.

She shook her head. "Yeah. They do a late brunch, so they should have people there now."

He rose out of his chair and smiled. "I love how you have a connection to food. You always know where to go for a meal."

She rolled her eyes and didn't tell him why she frequented restaurants as much as she did. That was her little secret, and only her family knew she couldn't even boil water.

"You're driving," he said, tossing her the keys. She caught them and followed him out the door. She was about to become part of a bad day for everyone at Fitzpatrick's.

She realized neither of them had said goodbye to Bryan when they stepped outside. They walked to the car, and once she started it up, she asked. "Why don't you like Bryan?"

"He's an asshole. I don't think he deserves to be detective, either. There have been complaints."

Eddie's wife was an Assistant DA, so he would have heard. "Yeah?"

"Not just from people he arrested. There were a few other uniforms who were uncomfortable working with him."

She thought about it as she drove. "I guess I could see it. He did not like when I beat him on a lot of stuff at the academy."

"I don't understand how you two dated." He shook his head.

"I was twenty-one."

He snorted. "Yeah, I didn't make the best decisions then either."

With a sigh, she pulled out into traffic. Today was definitely going to suck.

DECLAN ROLLED HIS SHOULDERS, trying to work out the knot between his shoulder blades. He really hated it when he got that tense. It was like a sixth sense thing. Bad things always happened when he felt like this. Of course, it might be that he had about three hours of sleep, and bouncing back after that amount of sleep wasn't something that had been easy since he'd hit thirty.

The worry came from Irene ghosting him. She had never been late for work since he'd hired her. The woman showed up early, stayed late, and was one of the best damned managers. When Adrian had called him to tell him she hadn't shown up, he'd been dead to the world and in the middle of the most amazing dream about Eileen.

Just thinking about it had his cock twitching and his entire body heating. Which, of course, was totally inappropriate. His brothers were right to chide him, though. He was taking too long before asking Eileen out and if he wasn't careful, some other guy would realize how wonderful she was.

"Hey, Declan, you said we're doing the red velvet pancakes today?" Sandy Howard asked him. His head chef was four years older than him, with three kids, a husband she adored, and a sarcastic sense of humor that matched his own. She'd been with him for over a year and ran the kitchen. Someday, he hoped he could promote her to take over everything, and he would just run the behind-the-scenes things. He loved to cook and plan menus, but he worked twelve-hour days at least six days a week and needed a break.

"Yeah. I also made extra cookie butter icing for the cakelets today."

"Fantastic. Thanks. Have you heard from Irene?"

He shook his head. "You?"

He knew the two women were close since they had hit it off after Irene started working at Fitzpatrick's.

"No. It's not like her, although she did have a date last night."

"She has a boyfriend?"

Sandy shrugged. "He was new. Maybe she overslept."

"Probably," he said, but he didn't tell her what he was really thinking. It was entirely out of character for her. "Just let me know if you hear from her."

She nodded, then hurried off to get to work.

That was when he noticed there was someone at the door. He was frowning when he realized who was there, and his entire body jumped back to life. Eileen was standing there next to an Asian man. Declan thought the guy might be her partner.

She cocked her head as she studied him through the front door, and he realized that he was staring at her like some moony-eyed goof.

He walked over and unlocked the door. He smiled, but neither of them returned it.

"Morning. Didn't expect to see you this early in the morning."

She was dressed in one of her badass suits. He knew many men didn't like them, but when Eileen strode into his bar for the first time, she had been wearing one. Each and every one of them fit her perfectly, and damn, but her ass looked good in them. She also looked like one tough detective in them, which was a turn-on for him. Not the fact that she was a detective but that she understood her worth.

"Can we talk?"

There was something in her voice, something...distant. He had never heard her speak like that before. Declan studied her and her partner. They wore the same grave expression and sported identical dark circles under their eyes. Whatever case she had last night must have been a bad one.

"Sure. Come on in. We can talk in my office."

They followed him back to his office, and he felt the weight of the stares. He had a few people in setting tables and making sure they were ready for the brunch crowd.

"Can I get you anything to drink?"

Both of them shook their heads.

"Please, have a seat."

They both sat, and Eileen waited for him to sit down.

"When was the last time you saw Irene Adams?"

That knot was back between his shoulders. *Dammit*.

"Yesterday afternoon. We shut down at two for the party prep, and she had the night off. She was supposed to be in today, but she never showed up. That's why I'm here."

"Declan, I'm sorry, but Irene was found murdered last night."

He blinked. "Murdered? You're sure?"

"What do you mean?" her partner asked.

Declan looked at him. "I mean, it wasn't an accident or anything?"

The man shook his head.

"Sorry, I forgot to introduce you to Eddie Francisco, my partner."

Declan nodded to the man. "Is there anything you can tell me? Anything I can do to help?"

"Irene has been working here for a few months, right?"

He swallowed, thinking about the day he'd hired the younger woman. She had been a go-getter with excellent references and shadows in her eyes.

"Yeah. Well, almost nine now. She's originally from Richmond." He closed his eyes, then opened them again. "Her parents are on an anniversary trip."

"We've already talked to them," her partner said. "You seem to know a lot about her."

Declan frowned. "She was my manager. Fitzpatrick's is a family business."

The man didn't look satisfied.

"Stop," Eileen said to him. "Declan has an alibi."

"You would know this how?" Francisco asked.

"Remember, I was here last night." She had been dancing in his arms when she got the call about Irene.

"Okay, do you know if she was seeing someone?"

He studied both of them. "I just heard she was dating someone new, but she was private about her personal life. She talked about her parents and brothers, but the guys were different. I know that she moved up here after a bad breakup."

"And you never met him?" Francisco asked.

"No. They broke up beforehand."

"Is there anyone she was really close to here? Someone she might have confided in?" Eileen asked.

"Sandy, my head chef. She's the one who insisted we start serving those red velvet pancakes for brunch you love so much."

"Is she here today?" Francisco asked.

He nodded. "I can get her for you."

"Thanks," Eileen said.

He rose out of his chair, but before he left them, Eileen stopped him.

"I'm really sorry, Declan."

"Yeah, me too."

He headed off to tell his people that one of their family was gone. His head pounded, and his heart hurt. Nothing about today was going to be good.

Eileen watched Sandy Howard as she absorbed the pain of the news. Again, it would probably be one of the worst days of her life. The African American woman had kind eyes, and Eileen remembered her wide smile last night. Every time she saw the woman, she had been smiling.

Some days, being a cop sucked.

"I'm sorry," Sandy said as she wiped away her tears.

"No problem," Eddie said in that soothing voice of his. He was much better at working with the criers than she was. She detested crying herself, so she knew it showed on her face. That's why she and Eddie were a good team. She kept them on track while he comforted the witnesses.

"Did she ever talk about her ex?" Eileen asked, trying her best to keep her voice gentle.

"Yeah. She'd had to move out of Richmond because of that asshole. She blocked his phone number, but she knew he was looking for her."

"He didn't know about her move to Baltimore?"

She shook her head. "I guess not at first. But she told me he found out about it through some mutuals. Some guy she worked with had been here to visit friends, and they came into Fitzpatrick's. She thought maybe he'd told him."

"Did she ever tell you his name?"

"Yeah. Bradley...no Brantley Brown." She rolled her hazel eyes. "I never met the guy, but he sounded like a real creep."

Eileen had to agree with her. And that is the second time the guy's name came up. They were definitely tracking that jerk down.

"But she was happy more recently, or at least she had started getting out there and dating. I encouraged her."

"Yeah? Did she have a steady guy?"

Sandy nodded. "I never met him, but she said he was a good guy. Had a steady job, which I think was a problem with the last guy. She said that he was an upstanding citizen."

Abusers often had issues with employment because of their aggression and temper. Not all, but a lot of them did, and Irene seemed to be an intelligent woman with a steady employment history. Another reason for an abuser like Brantley to get abusive—at least in his mind.

"Did she tell you his name?"

The other woman shook her head. "She did make a comment about bees. I don't know what she meant."

"If you think of anything, please call. Anything at all, even something small," Eddie said. "We'll let you get back to work."

"Oh, we're closing for the day."

Eileen blinked. "Declan closed for the day?"

Sandy nodded and sniffed into her tissue. "He has everyone hanging out so you can talk to them, but he said there was a death in the family, so we would close down today and tomorrow."

After she left them, Eddie whistled. "Your Declan definitely has his priorities straight. Tomorrow is no big deal, but closing today will lose him some money."

Eileen ignored the 'your' comment. "And last night for his parents' anniversary."

"So, we got this Brantley guy showing up twice in the investigation. We definitely need to track that asshole down."

"Yeah."

There was a knock on the door before it opened. Declan nodded at them.

"I assume you need to talk to the rest of the staff. Do you want me to send them in, one by one?"

"That would be great. Thanks, Declan."

He nodded and slipped out the door.

She stared at the spot where he'd stood, then shook herself. Eileen definitely needed some sleep.

When she looked at Eddie, he was smirking at her. Her face heated. God, she hated her fair skin. People could always tell when she was blushing.

"What?"

"You two ever going to go on a date?"

"Stop. You know I don't date much."

"Yeah. Maybe there's a reason for that. I mean, he *is* your Declan."

"I never said that. You said that."

"Guy watches everything you do."

She sighed. "He doesn't. And don't make him sound like a stalker. He's not."

The stalker would more likely be her. She was the one who came into the bar more often than not. And yes, it was because she loved his Shepherd's pie and also to see him. God, she was pathetic.

"Uh, Boss said you need to talk to us?"

Eileen glanced over and found a young Asian man with dark brown eyes dressed in white. One of the kitchen workers.

"Come on in," Eddie said with a smile.

She didn't have time to think about Declan or anything else. She had a murder to solve, and Eileen had a bad feeling about this one.

BY THE TIME Eileen and her partner finished their interviews, it was close to noon. Declan waited for them in the dining room.

Charlie came out, his expression telling Declan that he was gutted. They all were. Irene had been an odd manager, where almost everyone loved her, and it had nothing to do with her being a lax boss. She expected one hundred percent from everyone, but it was because she gave one hundred and ten percent. They respected her.

"You're working Tuesday, right?"

Charlie nodded.

"Don't worry. You will get your hourly rate for the two days."

"I'm not worried about that. Okay, yeah, that would be hard to lose, but it's just...Irene was the sweetest person I knew. Hard to think someone killed her."

Declan nodded. Everyone had said basically the same thing. "Get on home and be careful out there. See you Tuesday."

He locked the door behind Charlie just as Eileen and Francisco walked out from the back of the restaurant.

"I have a list of other employees if you want to talk to them. Most of them worked last night."

"Hey, why don't you text that to Detective O'Reilly?" her partner suggested.

Declan looked at Eileen. "I don't have the detective's number."

He had wanted to ask for it about a thousand times but had realized it just was never the right time.

"Oh," Francisco said. "No problem."

Then he rattled off the number.

"Okay. I'll get that to you as soon as I can."

"Thanks," Eileen said, her husky voice slinking down his spine. The woman got to him no matter what she did. Whether she was in one of her suits or that slinky dress. Declan could say that he would want her no matter how she was dressed.

"If you think of anything else, let us know," she said, heading to the door.

"I will."

"Thanks again, Declan. Sorry about Irene."

He nodded. Here, he was fantasizing about Eileen, and poor Irene had been killed.

After they left, he locked up and looked around the area. Thankfully, they served mainly cooked-to-order meals for brunch, so he would just take the cakes to the station house where his brothers worked. It took him about an hour to get everything taken care of and get to their station house. Both Emmett and Connal were working today.

"Hey, what are you doing here?" Emmett asked, and then his gaze landed on the box. "Cakes?"

Declan nodded. "Had to close up for today and tomorrow."

He set the box on the table in the break room. Declan might not have ever worked for the department, but his father and countless other relatives had actually worked in this station house. He knew it well and always felt nostalgic when he stopped by.

"Oh, are those cakes?" BeeBee said as she stepped into the break room. Emmett's best friend since about the age of five, BeeBee, real name Beatrice but she refused to acknowledge that name, Walters had spent most of her childhood at their house. At five foot seven, she was all leg and always moving. Blonde hair and brown eyes, she looked like the girl next door, which, for the Fitzpatricks, was true.

"Yeah," Emmett said. "Declan closed up for today. Why?"

He sighed and took a seat. "Irene's dead."

They all stopped what they were doing and looked at him.

"Dead?" Connal said. "How? Was she in a wreck?"

Declan shook his head. "She was murdered last night."

"Oh, damn," BeeBee said as she sat down beside him. "Do they know who did it? Was it that ex?"

"You knew about that?"

She shrugged. "I heard her and Sandy talking about the guy a week ago. Sounded like a complete jerk."

"You think all men are jerks," Emmett said.

"No. Most men are jerks, but this wasn't just being a jerk. I heard her say that the restraining order from Virginia wasn't valid here or something like that. So, no, not like guys I have dated, idiot."

Before they could start fighting as they always did, he said, "I'll let Eileen know."

Three sets of eyes settled on him, and there was a long beat of silence.

"What?"

"Why would you let Eileen know?" Connal asked.

"It's her case. That's why she was called away yesterday."

Connal and Emmett shared a look, and BeeBee looked anywhere but at him.

"What now?"

Emmett sighed and looked at Connal. "You should talk to him about his obsession with the detective."

"I don't have an obsession. Also, I don't like being talked about like I'm not here."

"He'll never accept that he is obsessed," Connal said, ignoring his comment. His brothers were jerks.

"That's because I'm not."

All three of them just stared at him. BeeBee let one eyebrow rise.

"I'm not. Anyone would find her attractive."

"True, but on the nights she's working, you keep your eye on the door," Connal said.

"I don't know when she's working."

Not really. There is a rhythm to her appearances at his restaurant. If more than three days passed without an appearance, he would often start to worry. That's all. Just...he needed to see her.

Oh, damn. He might be obsessed.

"See, this is what happens when you get hung up on someone," Emmett said. "You start to obsess about when they will show up and you even change plans in case this person might want to spend time with you. It's a sad sight."

"What would you know about that?" BeeBee asked, irritation threading her voice.

"What?" Emmett asked, utterly oblivious to BeeBee's moods, especially lately.

"Whatever," she said, without really answering his brother. She looked at Declan. "Ask her out. She likes you. You like her."

He rolled his shoulders about to ask her how to do that when she said, "Take her something to eat. You're good at that. And believe me, women could always do with a home cooked meal, especially when she has the kind of schedule she does."

"And what would you know about that?"

Emmett apparently wanted to be verbally beaten to a pulp.

"Why do you think I dated Patrick?"

Yeah, that had been fun. Patrick had been his sous chef before returning to the West Coast broken-hearted over his breakup with BeeBee.

"Because he cooked for you?" His brother sounded incredulous.

"That and he had very talented hands and, man...that tongue."

"Please, not in front of me," Declan said.

She smirked at him. "Take her food."

Then she rose out of her chair and left them, but Emmett... he was irritated. "You know she said that just to get me mad."

"Why would you get mad, Em?" Connal asked.

"I..." then his mouth snapped shut. "Whatever."

Then, he left Connal and Declan alone.

"Do you think he will ever get his head out of his ass?" Connal asked.

"Maybe?"

They all knew BeeBee and Em were half in love with each

other, but neither of them would act on it. He got it. They'd been friends for twenty years, so he understood why his brother didn't want to make a mistake with her.

"That doesn't sound like you're convinced."

He glanced at his brother. Connal was studying him in that way he had. He was the quiet brother who took time to notice things around him. Declan didn't like it one bit.

"What?"

"So, Eileen is the detective on the case?"

He nodded. If Connal was going to ask for her contact information, Declan would refuse and then punch him.

"When are you going to get *your* head out of your ass?"

The fact that he asked the same question about Emmett was not lost on Declan. He could pretend he didn't know what his brother was talking about. But Declan knew that was a stupid move.

"I've tried asking her out several times."

Connal frowned. "She turned you down?"

He shook his head. "I said I tried to ask her out. Didn't do it."

There was a beat of silence between them, filling the air as he listened to the other firemen move around the house. It was never quiet when you had a bunch of men and women who made their living by fighting fire.

"You're afraid to ask her out."

He sighed. "Not really, I just think it needs to be right. I know she has men hitting on her all the time."

He'd watched it in his bar. Since Fitzpatrick's was known more as a fireman bar, they didn't get a lot of cops. She was one of the few who was a regular, and men always tried to ask her out. Even some of the firemen he had known for years had a thing for her. The male badge bunnies were the worst. It was like the women who showed up at the bar looking for a night with a fireman. The job attracted them.

"Do what BeeBee told you to do."

He blinked, pulling himself back into the present. "What?"

"BeeBee said to take her food. That woman loves to eat. And I have a feeling none of those guys who hit on her do anything just for her."

"When did you get so wise?"

"I'm not. I'm just listening to a woman, which you should do. I bet both Wendy and Kaitlin would say the same thing. Also, I won't run to Ma about it, so I saved you that."

True. Wendy and his sister tended to tell their mother everything. "Okay. Well, I'm going to go now."

He knew exactly what to take her, and he had a few friends in her precinct who could tell him when she was on her way home.

THE FITZPATRICKS

Six

"Face it, we have diddly shit," Eddie said.

It was late...well, past time for them to go home, but neither one of them was ready for that. It annoyed her that there wasn't a witness or a traffic cam...nothing to point to the killer. She had an ex—who they were hunting down—and a mystery man. That was it. And they had nothing else to go on until they could interview both of them. Going through her phone had given them little to nothing.

"We do. But we've dealt with this before."

He nodded. She saw the dark circles under his eyes, the way his shoulders sagged. They were both exhausted.

"No one seemed to have a problem with her at work," she mused. "But looks can be deceiving. We should probably triple-check those alibis for people who weren't at the party."

"Yeah. We can do that tomorrow, though. By then, we should have more on the tox screen and her phone data."

The warrant to trace her phone's ping had come through pretty fast. Having a woman murdered in a high-traffic area where a lot of tourists visit definitely got things rolling. Unfortunately, there was a significant backlog of cases, so they wouldn't get that information until tomorrow.

She sighed. The long day and late night were wearing her down. "You're right."

"Hey," he said, and she looked at him. "We'll get the information."

She nodded. Irene's parents had shown up to identify her. It was always hard for Eileen to deal with that element of a case. Well, just about every cop hated that part of the job. There were a few whom it didn't bother, and she avoided those weirdos.

"I say we call it a day. Come back tomorrow morning fresh. We'll have the phone pings by then, and we can start hunting down her movements from Saturday night."

She nodded again. "That sounds like a plan."

Eileen dropped down in her chair. She had other things she could work on, like the Norma Wilson case for her mother. The similarities were a little too much to ignore.

"You need to go home."

She looked up at Eddie. He looked about as tired as she felt. Dark circles bruised the skin beneath his brown eyes. Eileen was pretty sure he looked better than she did.

"I was just going to—"

"You need to go home," Eddie said, then glanced behind her. Casually, she turned around and saw Bryan making his way through the myriad of desks in the bullpen.

"Okay, you're right."

Her stomach grumbled as she stood, and Eddie laughed.

"What will you do since your chef is closed for the night?"

Peanut butter. That was her go-to when she didn't feel like cooking, which was a lot of the time.

"Don't worry. I got it."

"Hey," Bryan said. He smiled, showing off his newly capped teeth. God, she had been stupid when she was twenty-two. Really, really stupid.

"Hey."

She did not encourage talk, but since he was the nephew of the deputy police commissioner, she'd always played nice after their breakup. Or as nice as she could with a sociopath.

"Closing up early?"

It was after seven on a Sunday. Both she and Eddie had worked until almost dawn, then put in a full eight hours. This butthead was annoying, and she wanted to punch him.

Eileen, don't hit the deputy's nephew, no matter how much he deserves it.

"Yeah, you could say that." Eddie was the one who answered him. Eddie was one of those guys who was nice to everyone. Not just to Bryan.

She shut down her computer, then grabbed her purse and gun. "We're beat after last night and this morning. Techs are working on stuff for us, but we won't see anything until tomorrow. Have a good night."

She joined Eddie, feeling the heat of Bryan's stare as they left him there.

"Listen, I get that you were young when you first dated him."

"Yeah, stupid. Thought he would be like the rest of my police family."

"You are going to have to tell him to bugger off."

She laughed. Eddie's wife spent part of her childhood in England, and sometimes, he would slip into their idioms.

"Watching some BBC lately?"

65

"Yeah. We're gonna have to take a trip back there soon. Marguerite's been missing it."

She could get that. She'd miss Baltimore if she moved away. Lots of people would question her sanity, but it was home.

"I'm just saying, you'll have to kick that weirdo puppy to the curb."

"Don't say that."

"He *is* weird."

"No, don't equate him to a puppy."

He snorted, then grew serious. "I think that he has a fixation on you."

She stopped by her car. Eddie was parked next to her. "It isn't romantic or even just sexual. He's still pissed I made detective before him."

"Asshole."

"Exactly. Kiss that baby for me."

"I will."

She slipped into her car. When she reached the exit, she almost turned towards Fitzpatrick's before remembering it was closed. The thought of fast food nauseated her, so peanut butter it was. As she drove, she tried to push the idea of the case away, of the similarities to the cold case. Could it be that someone was trying to emulate the original murder? Or was it a coincidence?

She shook her head. Coincidences take too much planning, and this one looked like it. Good girl left in an alley, stabbed, stripped...left next to the trash. Was the original assessment wrong? Was the woman killed in '87 younger than they'd initially thought?

Those thoughts rolled around in her head until she pulled into her driveway. That's why she didn't see him until she grabbed her purse and gun. He was sitting on her stoop with a container beside him. Eileen blinked, trying to figure out if she was imagining her favorite chef sitting there. Nope. He was there.

Slipping out of her car, she took her time walking toward him.

"Whatcha doing here, Declan?"

He cocked his head. "A little bird told me you were on your way home. I thought you could do with something good to eat."

He tapped the container beside him. Warmth filled her chest. She couldn't remember the last time someone took care of her. Or even thought about things like feeding her.

"Yeah?"

She couldn't fight the smile as happiness filled her.

He nodded. "Not to be presumptuous, but I brought enough for two."

Another kind of warmth filled her, slipping through her blood and heating her from within. Just the thought of eating a meal together, alone...the intimacy made her hot and worried at the same time. It was a weird feeling.

"Or not?"

She shook her head. "Yes. I would like for you to join me."

Then, he smiled. It was slow, sexy, and his eyes brightened as he studied her. Her breath tangled in her throat as she studied him. His hair was down tonight, which he usually kept up at the bar. Man buns were not her thing, but on him...it made her smile.

"Let's go in."

He stood, grabbed the container, then stepped aside for her. She had danced with him less than twenty-four hours ago. She knew how big he was, but...this was different. It was just the two of them.

"Hey, Eileen," Mrs. Kilpatrick called out.

Okay, not alone. She glanced at the stoop next door. Rosemary Kilpatrick was in her seventies and independent as the day was long. She stood just under five feet and probably weighed about one hundred pounds soaking wet. She wore a short housecoat and rollers in her thinning hair, but that was normal at any time of day.

"Hey, Mrs. Kilpatrick."

"I wanted to make sure you were okay." The stern look she gave Declan had Eileen biting back a laugh.

"Mrs. Kilpatrick, this is Declan Fitzpatrick."

"Oh, you know him?"

"Yes, and he brought me food."

Her gaze raked over him. "Are you one of Deirdre's boys?"

"Yes, ma'am," Declan rumbled. He had one of those wonderfully deep baritones. It always slipped beneath her heart every time he spoke.

"You tell her Rosemary Kilpatrick said hello." He nodded, and then Mrs. Kilpatrick's gaze turned to Eileen. "You need rest, girl."

"Well, I would get some after the yummy meal waiting for me, but some nosey Nora is keeping me out here."

The gleam in the older woman's eyes told Eileen she was amused. "Don't sass your elders."

Then she turned and walked into her house.

"Sorry about that," Eileen said as she continued to stand there. He sure was pretty.

"Eileen?"

"Yeah?"

"Thanks for the compliment, but maybe we should get out of this chill?"

Her face flushed. Oh, damn, she said that out loud.

"Don't be embarrassed. I think you're pretty, too."

She rolled her eyes. After unlocking the door, she stepped aside, but he shook his head. "Ladies first."

Such a gentleman. Of course, all the Fitzpatrick boys were like that. She had a feeling Deirdre pounded those lessons into them.

"I'll need to warm this up a little bit."

She nodded and showed him to her kitchen. She wasn't a cook, but the kitchen was made for one. It had a six-burner gas stove, a large island, and tons of glass-fronted cabinets.

"Wow, nice."

"Don't be fooled. I burn water when I try to boil it."

He glanced at her with a lopsided grin that had her curling her toes inside her shoes.

"Then it's a good thing I'm here. Did you want to get out of your work clothes?"

Her eyes narrowed. "Excuse me?"

His laugh filled the kitchen. "Not like that, although if you offer, I would definitely be okay with it. You've worked a long day, and I figured you would prefer to get into some other clothes. I'm the same way when I get home."

She shook her head. "Yeah, that does sound good. What do you need from me?"

His eyes heated. "So much, but for the moment, just some pots."

For a second, she wondered about the first part of his comment, but she was too tired to think. Besides, she was probably reading more into it because she was exhausted.

"In the cabinet next to the stove."

He nodded.

"I'll be right back."

"No rush. This will take about ten or fifteen minutes to heat it up. Brought some of that bread you like too."

She almost moaned. She loved the garlicky crusty loaf they served with their soups and stews.

"Be right back."

She hurried up the stairs and to her room. She stripped out of her shirt and realized she smelled of stale coffee and too many hours at work. Since he said it would be a few minutes, she decided to take a quick shower. She might look like death, but at least she wouldn't smell like it.

THE MINUTE DECLAN heard the shower come on, he closed his eyes. He would not think of Eileen naked with the water dripping off her—

His eyes shot open, and he glanced down. Yep, that's all it took. An image of her in the shower and his unruly cock was raring to go. Hell, the moment she drove up, Declan had to count backward from ten to get himself under control. Granted, he had to do it three times before it worked.

He grabbed a pot—they would have to talk about her cookware because this one was dented and older than dirt—and filled it with the Irish stew she loved. In the past, he hadn't knowingly cooked for her. Tonight, he had been dedicated to making this the best stew she had ever had.

After setting that on the burner, he tossed the bread into the oven to heat it up. The kitchen filled with the scents of his cooking. Something settled in his chest. It was the same feeling he got the first time he had stepped into the kitchen at Fitzpatrick's. He grabbed a couple of bowls, along with small plates and thankfully, she had butter. The woman really didn't have any food in her refrigerator. There had been a half-empty bottle of Chardonnay, two containers of yogurt—both out of date—and a six-pack of Guinness.

His phone went off with his mother's ringtone. He would ignore it, but he knew better than to do that, especially after what happened.

"Hey, Ma."

"Hey, yourself. I thought you might stop by tonight."

He had thought about it, but that was before he started cooking for Eileen. Everything else in the world seemed to melt away. All that mattered was what he had been doing for her. Declan wasn't sure how he felt about that.

"I made dinner for a friend since we were closed tonight."

"A friend?"

This was the part he was uncomfortable with. His mother didn't pry—especially in comparison to Joey Santini. Of course, there was a good chance that no one got into your business like Brando's aunt. The CIA didn't have people as talented as Joey when she ws on the trail of information. But, he figured it was better to just tear that bandage off.

"Yep. In fact, I ran into someone you might know. Rosemary Kilpatrick."

"Oh, God," she said with a chuckle. "Yeah, I know Rosemary. I went to school with her daughter Phyllis."

"Well, she said hello."

"I'll have to check on her then. I know she lost Lloyd a

couple of years ago. Phyllis lives down in DC with her husband."

He released an uneasy breath. Now that he got his mother onto the thought of Rosemary, he might have avoided discussing who he was cooking for. Other than work, he didn't go out of his way to cook for anyone but family. It had been at least three years since he'd been involved, and his ex had been a calorie counter. Not that anything was wrong with that, but she had an aversion to the idea of him cooking for her.

After her stunning looks and that no-nonsense attitude, he had been amazed by Eileen's food obsession. The woman was compact, but she ate a lot of food.

"Well, I'll be home tomorrow if you want to come over."

"I will."

"Say hello to Eileen for me."

"Wait, what makes you think I'm at Eileen's?"

She chuckled. "I know she lives next door to Rosemary. We've had long conversations about how nosey that old woman is. Love you."

"Love you, Ma."

He hung up right as he heard the floor creak behind him. When he turned, every thought he had in his brain bled away. God, she was gorgeous. No makeup, just an old FBI shirt he was sure she got from one of her brothers because it was so big. The baggy sweats showed no hint of her figure. Her feet were bare, showing off red toenails.

"I hope you're okay with me dressing down."

He'd rather she be naked, but Declan decided to keep that to himself.

"I'm fine with however you want to dress."

She cocked her head and studied him for a long moment. "I believe that."

Declan frowned. "Why would I lie about that?"

"Lots of guys do."

The alarm he had set on his phone went off, and he took his attention away from the totally delectable woman in front of him and retrieved the bread. "Have a seat, detective, and tell me what guys lie about."

She grabbed a glass and filled it with ice and water. "Want anything? I have Guinness."

"Water's fine."

He did not need to add alcohol to the evening. He was barely keeping it together as it was.

Once they were settled at the kitchen bar, she sighed. "This was an awful day. Thank you for this."

He studied her for a long moment. "No leads?"

She shook her head as she tore off a piece of bread and dipped it in the stew. Once it passed her lips, she moaned. Damn. He didn't need that sound knocking around in his brain.

"I can't really say anything. Open investigation."

He nodded and understood. It didn't make him feel any better, but her taking it so seriously meant the world to him. She was a first-class cop. She had proven that when Wendy had had a stalker.

She took a sip of her stew, then she slanted a look at him.

"What?"

"Her parents told me you footed the bill for their hotel room."

It would be a long time before he would get their devastated looks out of his head. "It was the least that I could do."

"No," she shook her head before facing him. "It isn't the least you could do. Sending a card. That would be the least you could do. You made sure that they had arrangements. I know there's so much to deal with in a situation like this. Having one less thing to worry about is golden."

"You speak from experience."

"No." She turned to face her food again. "Not personally. But I've had to deal with family members. It never gets easier telling people. At least, those who aren't suspects."

He hadn't even thought about that, probably because Irene's parents were not suspects. "Does that happen a lot with family? They're suspects?"

Declan knew that a lot of entertainment might have that as a plot point, but he always wondered how close to reality it was.

"More often than not, it's someone very close to the victim."

He nodded and let her eat for a few moments. The quiet didn't bother him, not with Eileen there, but also the cozy feel of the house.

"Let's leave that alone so you don't compromise the investigation's integrity."

"Okay."

"Tell me why you were surprised by my reaction to how you're dressed."

"Not important."

There was something in her voice, something that told him that this was something she'd dealt with in the past. "Oh, I think it's very important."

"Listen."

"I'm all ears."

She nibbled on her lower lip, which made him want to kiss

her. God, this woman was driving him insane, but the truth was that she had no idea. At least Declan didn't think she did.

"Guys tend to get off on me being a cop."

"Okay."

"They ask me out and seem to think I should act differently. When we date or spend time together, they start harping on me not dressing like a woman."

"Bullshit."

She cut him a look. "It's true."

"Oh, no, I believe you. I just think it's bullshit."

"Oh."

"For the record, I love the way you were dressed last night, and I really love your pantsuits."

Her brow creased. "You do not."

He nodded. "You are put together perfectly, Detective O'Reilly. And those pants you wear for work? They show off that world-class ass of yours."

Her face flushed, and for a second, he thought he might have overstepped. Other women, he knew what to say, but he often felt as if he were out of his depth with Eileen.

"Sorry."

Her gaze shot to his. She had the most amazing eyes. Dark, with golden flecks within the iris. The freckles across the bridge of her nose were cute and sexy at the same time.

"You didn't mean it?"

"No, I meant it." He shoved a hand through his hair. "I thought maybe you were offended."

"No," she said as she turned to face him completely. Lifting a hand, she took hold of his. "I wasn't because it's the truth."

There was a long beat of silence. The laughter bubbled up.

"You are one of a kind, Eileen."

Another blush stole over her cheeks. Adorable. He wanted more...so much more. Declan wasn't sure where this would go, but he was sure it would be more serious than a casual relationship.

He could tell she was barely awake by the time she finished eating. Declan rose and took the bowls against her protests.

"You cook. I clean."

He shook his head. "You're falling asleep as you sit there. Let me do this."

His mother had always called him a caregiver. It was partially what drove him to cook in the first place. He loved giving nourishment to people he cared about.

They spoke of nothing of much importance as he cleaned off the bowls and put them in her dishwasher. When he was done, he turned to face her, resting his weight against the counter. She was doing the same against the island.

"Thank you," she said. Drowsiness filled her voice, and he knew it was time to leave. "I'll have to pay you back for that."

This was the chance he had waited for. "Go out with me."

She blinked. "Out?"

"Like on a date."

Again, she was nibbling on her bottom lip. "You want to go on a date with me?"

She sounded like she didn't believe him. "Yes."

"Okay."

The fast reply had his head almost spinning. "Wednesday night? It's the one night I'm off this week."

She nodded. "Although, don't be surprised if I have to cancel."

"Already trying to let me off easy."

Her mouth curved. "There is nothing easy about you. I

meant that I sometimes get called in like I did on Saturday night."

"No problem."

She sighed.

"What? What did that mean?"

"It's just...okay, guys always say that but then they get pissed when I have to cancel."

He stepped forward and took her hand. "I understand. Remember, family of firemen. I'm the one weirdo."

She shook her head. "Thank God because I wouldn't date you otherwise."

He chuckled. "Good to know. You look dead on your feet."

"Way to romance me, Fitzpatrick."

"Beautiful but tired. Come on, walk me to the door."

He held her hand as he walked to the door. After pulling on his coat, he faced her again. The hall light wasn't on, but her porch light was. The dim light hit her perfectly, and he couldn't stop himself from leaning forward to brush his mouth against hers.

It was simple, just lips against lips, but then she opened her mouth, and Declan lost a little control. He slipped his tongue into her mouth as he crowded her up against the wall. He skimmed his hands down that tight body of hers, enjoying her slight curves. It took every bit of his control to pull back. They were both breathing heavily.

Eileen lifted her hand to brush her fingers over her mouth. "Wow."

She said the word in a hushed whisper.

"Yeah, wow."

He swooped in for another kiss, then stepped away. If he

didn't leave right then, he knew he wouldn't make it out of her house.

"Let me know if you can't make it Wednesday night. We'll reschedule."

She nodded and watched him as he ambled down the stairs. "Lock the door, Eileen."

She rolled her eyes. "I've been caring for myself for a while, Fitzpatrick."

"Time to get used to someone else helping."

He stood by his car and waited. With a huff, she shut the door. Declan was humming when he slipped into his car. He might have just figured out how to handle Eileen.

HE STOOD ACROSS THE STREET, his concentration on the house in front of him. He watched as the giant put his paws on Eileen O'Reilly. The fucker had no right to do that. When he had seen her show up at the crime scene the night before, it was a sign he couldn't ignore. But this...this was unacceptable.

He watched as the idiot drove away. He didn't know the man well, but most people in Baltimore knew the Fitzpatricks. How could she let a man from that family touch her?

He drew in a deep breath...calming his nerves. He needed something else to gain her attention, something that would make Eileen understand that they were meant to be together.

Seven

E
ileen smeared a bit of lip gloss on her mouth, then took in her appearance. It wasn't Wednesday like they had planned, but the following Monday. There had been a significant gang bust on Wednesday afternoon, which required all hands on deck. Declan hadn't complained. He just told her Monday would work for him.

Now, she was nervous. He would be there in less than five minutes and her stomach kept turning over. She hadn't been this nervous about a date in...she couldn't remember. Maybe ever? There was just something about Declan that made her anxious, but not in a scary way. Eileen just never knew what to make of him.

Her phone vibrated, and she saw her mother's face. This was going to be tricky. She loved her mother, and she did stay out of her business, but she would pick up on something being off tonight.

Pulling in a deep breath, she clicked to answer.

"Hey, Ma."

"What's wrong?"

"Nothing's wrong. Why would you say that?"

A beat of silence went by. "Okay, I'll let that go. I just wanted to see if you wanted to grab a bite to eat tonight. Your father is out with his old cop buddies, and I felt like a pizza."

"I have a date."

Another beat of silence.

"Not another cop."

She frowned. "No. You know I don't date cops."

"You dated Bryan."

"That was at the academy, and it taught me enough about guys I work with. Anyway, he'll be here soon."

"You might as well tell me."

"Tell you what?"

"Tell me who it is. Eddie will tell me."

"No grilling Eddie," she said, although she was smiling. Eddie's mother was kind of scary, so he had a rational fear of women—his words, not hers. It was probably why they worked so well together.

"You know that boy tells me stuff without me asking."

"Fine. Declan Fitzpatrick."

The silence almost vibrated over the phone. "The one who owns the bar and grill?"

"Yes."

"He comes from a firemen family." She said it like they were completely different creatures. The truth was, she never understood the rivalry. Eileen always felt like they were two sides of the same coin. Of course, it was more of a dick-measuring thing, and since she didn't have one, Eileen figured that was why she couldn't truly understand it.

She rolled her eyes. "Yes, but he's a chef and cooks for me."

"Good because you can*not* cook."

"Hey!"

"Just telling you the truth, baby girl. Your talent lies elsewhere. Where are you going?"

"Not sure. He said casual and told me to wear jeans."

"So outside."

Or he liked her ass in her jeans, but she decided not to tell her mom that.

"Listen, he's going to be here any moment."

"Okay. Have a good time, but not too good."

Another eye roll from Eileen. "Don't worry. I'm saving myself for marriage."

There was no doubting the sarcasm in her voice.

"Why would you do that?" Yes, her mother had been unconventional for a girl who went to a Catholic elementary school. "I just meant no drinking and driving."

Yes, Eileen was a cop, so she should know better. But her Uncle Jerry had been a cop who was killed in a drunk driving incident. He was the drunk driver. Thankfully, it had been a one-car accident, and he had been alone.

"No problem. I'm not driving. Love you."

"Love you."

Once she hung up, she looked at herself again in the mirror and nodded. She was sure she would have an amazing time, and Declan had said he liked her style.

Just as she had calmed her nerves with that pep talk, the doorbell rang, and butterflies sprang to life.

Get yourself together, O'Reilly.

Drawing in a deep breath, she walked to the door. Before she could open it, she heard Declan talking to someone.

"You better treat that girl right."

Oh, God, that Mrs. Kilpatrick was a menace.

"Yes, ma'am."

"Thought you spent the night the other night."

"Nope. Just brought the detective some Shepherd's pie. She'd had a long day."

And just like that, a lump rose in her throat. Yes, she'd had a long day last Sunday. But he had also had a long day. It wasn't easy dealing with grief. To have someone who paid enough attention to her to know when she needed support. It wasn't the fault of those around her. Eileen knew it was her own doing. It came from being the only girl in her family. Add in her job, and it was a mess in her head. She knew she could ask for support, but her pride kept her from doing it.

Somehow, Declan had understood just what she needed that night. No more. No less. He'd asked her out, but he hadn't acted like she owed him anything for the kindness he had shown her. Her heart turned over.

She pushed those thoughts aside because otherwise, she would stand there for hours mooning over the man who was presently being accosted by her neighbor.

Rolling her shoulders, she opened the door. Declan had been facing her neighbor's stoop, saying something, but it didn't register with Eileen. Instead, the man was all she saw. He'd dressed casually, a pair of jeans and a dress shirt. That wasn't what held her attention. It was his hair.

God, the man had hair like Thor. It was long and thick with just the right amount of curl. Never before had she fantasized about running her fingers through a man's hair, but she'd had insane dreams about being wrapped in those long strands. When he turned to face her, he was smiling, his eyes dancing with humor. It quickly dissolved as his gaze traveled down her body, then back up again. Heat filled his expression, and her entire body shimmered in response. She had seen lust in a man's gaze before, but there was something different with Declan.

She looked down at her outfit, then back up at him. "You said casual."

"I did."

"Is there something wrong?"

He shook his head. "I forgot that you stun me no matter what you wear."

Her stomach filled with butterflies. Again.

"Let me grab my coat and purse."

He nodded and waited. He didn't try to get into her house or insist on getting them for her. Yes, some women liked that, and there was nothing wrong with that. Declan seemed to understand her need for control.

Once her jacket was on, she set her alarm and stepped out on the stoop. Turning, she locked the door.

"You smell nice," Declan murmured.

She faced him with a smile. "Thank you."

"Night, Mrs. Kilpatrick."

She waved them off as Declan led her to his car. After opening the door for her, he waited for her to be seated before shutting the door and then hurrying around to the other side.

As he drove, she waited for him to tell her where they were going. When he didn't, she decided to rip that Band-Aid off.

"So, where are we going tonight?"

He glanced over at her, a small smile playing about his mouth. This man and his smiles.

"It's a surprise."

She wanted to growl. "Good. I like surprises."

He laughed as he turned onto a familiar street. "No, you don't."

She smiled because she didn't. She frowned when he drove by his restaurant and hooked a left on the side street. He then turned into a parking lot behind his restaurant. She had known it was there, but it was for employees and residents.

"You brought me to your restaurant."

"Nope."

Then, the maddening man slipped out of the car and walked around the back. He opened the door just as she was undoing her seatbelt.

Declan held out his hand and waited. Eileen didn't hesitate, anticipation simmering within her. She might not like surprises, but she was always curious to discover things. And that included what was going on tonight.

There were two doors in the back of the restaurant. One was clearly for the kitchen because of the signs about deliveries. He unlocked the other door and held it open for her.

As she stepped inside, she blinked.

"Oh, damn, I meant to leave the light on."

Declan stepped around her, his arm brushing against her, his tantalizing scent wrapping around her. Eileen fought the need to lean closer and get a bigger sniff. The light let her see the stairs to her left. She looked back over her shoulder.

"I take it we go up the stairs?"

He nodded. She started up the stairs and thought she heard a groan behind her. Frowning, she continued on. When they reached the top floor, she stepped into an apartment. It was more like a loft with an open floor plan. There was a bank of windows that looked out on the street below. There were plants everywhere, some herbs and some regular plants. As she stepped into the space further, she noticed the oversized leather sectional. Pictures littered every surface, from the credenza and side tables to the walls. His family was there for everyone to see. This area probably got fantastic morning light since the windows faced east.

As she turned, she noticed a door against the one wall and assumed it was the bedroom. Also, something smelled...amazing. And she knew it wasn't from downstairs. It smelled like...

"I heard that you like spaghetti and meatballs."

She glanced over at him and blinked. "I do. Who did you hear that from?"

"I do not reveal my sources. I need to start some water going on the stove, then we can get some wine and go upstairs."

"Upstairs?"

He nodded to the far left of the room. There was another staircase.

"Can you drink?"

"Yeah, I'm supposed to be off tomorrow."

"Are you okay with a cab? It will go best with the red sauce."

She snorted. "Yeah. I'm not about to say no to the chef who knows how to pair food with drink."

He poured the wine. "Do you want to eat right now?"

"It smells like it's almost done."

"The sauce has been simmering all day. It's the reason pasta was a good idea, it cooks fast. I also have some antipasto to eat."

Her mouth watered. She loved Irish food but had a true love affair with Italian food. So much so that she had an Italian trip savings. She planned to eat her way through Italy one noodle at a time. That is, if she could ever find the time to go.

"That sounds amazing."

He pulled out a tray. "Grab your drink, and we can go upstairs."

"I had no idea you lived up here."

"Not a lot of people do," he said. "The employees know not to tell anyone. At first, I did it because of the savings. When I opened the restaurant, I had to sink all my money into it. I worked on the apartment, thinking I would rent it out later, but I like the idea of being so close to work. I don't have to rush anywhere."

The moment Eileen stepped onto the roof, she blinked again. It looked out over the city and to the harbor, lights sparkling in the dark night. He had set it up nicely, with a scattering of tables, one that had candles on it. Declan set the plate down on it and removed the plastic.

"This is amazing," she said, looking around the area. A couch was on the far end, along with Edison lights strung overhead.

When he didn't say anything, she faced him once more. Was he blushing? "The view or the food?"

"All of it," she said with a laugh. "Now, watch me destroy this platter of food."

Do not embarrass yourself.

It was the same thing he kept telling himself in his head over and over, trying his best to keep himself from grabbing her hand and pledging his love to her. Yes, some people would think it was fast, but he had been mooning over her for a year.

He was plating up their food as she descended the stairs.

"I was bringing this up to you," he said. He wanted to pamper her and show her he could also do heavy lifting in the relationship. Not that they had a relationship. Not really.

"I was going to grab the wine, and I knew you would have your hands full."

He smiled. "Sure."

She did just that, and then they went up the stairs. Once again, he followed her and had to bite back a groan. The woman had the most amazing ass. Full, heart-shaped, and those jeans did not hide anything. Each time he followed her up the stairs, he had to order his body back under control. They settled back in the seats beneath the stars.

He waited, pretending to take a massive amount of time to twirl his pasta around his fork. Anticipation skated along his nerves. Never before had it been this important to impress someone with his cooking. The simple pomodoro sauce was one of the first non-Irish dishes he'd learned to make as a kid.

Eileen moaned when she tasted the pasta. "Why don't you serve this in the restaurant?"

He quirked an eyebrow, trying to tamp down on his need. Her enjoyment was the only aphrodisiac he needed. Well, and her. Just her breathing turned him on.

"Irish bar and grill, O'Reilly."

She chuckled as she scooped up another forkful. After swallowing, she apparently realized that he wasn't eating.

"What? Do I have food on my face?" She rolled those amazing eyes.

"No. Just…"

Declan didn't know how much he should reveal to her.

"Just?"

Now, she wasn't eating. She put her fork down.

"I'm discovering feeding you to be overwhelming."

She cocked her head to one side. "Overwhelming?"

Nerves had him hesitating, but he decided not to be a wuss and just blurt it out.

"I get enjoyment out of feeding you."

"Hmm." That was all she said, but she picked up her fork again. He joined her in eating.

"I guess that's a chef thing?"

He shrugged one shoulder. "I guess. I do like cooking for people I care about."

"Oh," she said, but he felt he had disappointed her somehow.

"But..." he sighed. "There is something different about making something I know is for you."

She blinked at him. "Different?"

"Yeah."

"Don't tell me you haven't used food to seduce women before me. That would be a lie."

He felt heat fill his face. She laughed out loud, the joyous sound surrounding him. Declan didn't mind the embarrassment because Eileen rarely let loose like that.

"I have, but not like this."

Her smile faded. "Oh, okay."

Then he realized she took it the wrong way. "No."

"No?"

God, this woman. He always sounded like an idiot around her. Declan figured it had more to do with the fact that he was trying to operate his brain with half the amount of blood. The rest of it drained to his groin.

"You're different. It's not just about seduction with you. I mean...don't get me wrong. Seduction is definitely on the table."

"Good to know."

That pulled a chuckle out of him even as his eager dick twitched. "But I don't just want to seduce you."

Now, she looked...he couldn't come up with one word to describe it. It was a mixture of worry and hope.

"And I'm sorry if I'm being blunt. I don't have finesse when it comes to you, Eileen. I did all this up here for you, and I only do that for family."

"Wait, are you telling me you never bring women up here?"

He shook his head. "I tend to avoid having women over at my apartment, let alone up here. It's my business, which could go wrong if you know what I mean."

"So this," she said, waving her hand around before she picked up her wine glass, "is just for me."

"And family."

There was a long silence as she sipped her wine and set her glass down. A smile curved her lips. It wasn't a grin, but one of those secret smiles women gave that told you that you had finally done something right.

"Good to know."

His chest warmed at those three words.

* * *

HE FOLLOWED the woman down the street. She was so freaking high she didn't notice him, but even if she had been sober, she probably wouldn't have seen him. He was good at lurking in the shadows. The week had passed, and no other woman had presented herself, or at least not until tonight. Until he found out that *his* Eileen was with Declan Fitzpatrick. Again.

He felt the cold press of the knife against the palm of his

hand. It matched the last one...part of a set. He knew it was risky to copy a murder from the 80s. Still, everyone knew about Eileen's infatuation with the old murder. This was how she would see they were meant to be together.

As his prey slipped into the alley, he sighed with relief. It wasn't busy on Fleet Street, thanks to the chilly rain, but he had not wanted to have this woman screaming and attracting attention.

From her dress, she was either working the streets or had no taste in fashion. She was also skinner than he liked his women, but sometimes, the need to kill was greater than having the perfect prey.

She stumbled and cussed. Fucking junkie. At least she would turn out to be easy to take down, not like Irene.

He pulled his knife out of his coat pocket. Excitement filled him, almost leaving him dizzy. Eileen would understand the connection.

Eight

They cleaned the dishes together. Like they were some old married couple who had celebrated together or just had dinner together. Usually, domesticity freaked Eileen out. Guys who pushed for more always seemed to leave her nervous. But here she was on her first date with Declan, and she was happy to hang out in the kitchen laughing over sibling stories.

"Are you telling me that you let Aeden think Kaitlin was the one who tattled on him sneaking out?"

He chuckled as he handed her one last dish to dry. "Yep. And to this day, he still thinks it."

"How long ago was that?"

"Twenty years."

"Damn, you definitely know how to keep things in the vault. I guess we have that in common."

He turned off the water as she dried the dish. "Yeah. It was hard being the only girl and the one non-twin. They had their own secret language beyond just being boys."

"And being a woman in a male-dominated field."

She glanced up at him, a little surprised.

"What? I know that has to be hard. I know it is for BeeBee."

"Oh, the girl your brother has a crush on?"

"Yes!" He laughed. "See, they both act like they aren't hot for each other, but they are." He shook his head. "Not that I can talk."

"What do you mean?"

"I've been trying to ask you out for at least six months."

She almost dropped the dish she had been drying. She carefully set it down and looked at him. "What?"

Again, his cheeks turned ruddy. She had to admit that a blushing Declan was just as cute as a regular Declan. Either way, she wanted him.

"Listen, this is embarrassing, but what I said about the food was true. I've been trying to get to you since I met you."

"During your sister-in-law's investigation?"

He nodded. She frowned. "Declan, you don't have to make up stories."

"I'm not. I promise." He shoved a hand through his hair. "It's embarrassing to admit that for the first time since I was about fourteen, I lacked the nerve to ask you out."

"But you finally did?"

He nodded as he raised his hand to brush the back of his fingers over her cheek. "I'd have a plan, and then I would look into your eyes and lose every word I had memorized to say to you."

"Uh. Same."

"Really?"

She nodded. "I've also been busy with getting a new partner." Her last partner had retired, and she and Eddie had been getting to know each other. "But I knew I was using that as an excuse."

He cupped her jaw with one hand as he moved closer.

Close enough to kiss.

It was the one thought she had the second or two before she felt his mouth brush over hers. She knew that he had probably planned a simple kiss, one that hinted at the passion they shared but kept banked. But that was all it took. One...two...then something changed. Heat coursed through her entire body as her head spun. Declan slanted his mouth over hers and deepened the kiss. His tongue stole inside. Eileen could taste the wine...and him. All Declan. She slipped her hands up to his shoulders as he pulled her closer. As he turned them so that her back was to the counter, their bodies pressed together.

Oh, hello. He was definitely hard. Her nipples pebbled, ached. Before she was ready, he wrenched himself away. They were both breathing heavily.

"Damn," he said. He took a step away, his eyes wide. She immediately felt cold. Lifting her hand, she touched her lips. "Sorry."

"Why?"

His gaze connected with hers. "I was a little rough there."

She laughed. It was all she could do because he always made her feel that way. Around him, even if she had the worst day, the world seemed brighter and lighter.

"In case you didn't notice, I liked it."

He drew in a breath, then released it. "I was trying to go slow."

"Again, why? It's not like we just met." Eileen reached up to grab his shirt and tug him back. "And it's not like I asked you to stop."

Then she kissed him again. She wasn't sure that she would ever be this close to him and be able not to kiss him. Now that she knew how he tasted, she was afraid she might have just turned into an addict.

Again, he pulled away, but at least this time, he didn't step away from her. "This wasn't my plan."

She frowned at him. "You had a plan?"

This man was talking about plans and what he expected, and she just wanted in his pants.

He shook his head. "I didn't bring you here for this."

Heat flushed her face, and not because of the arousal. No, this was embarrassment. Before she could slip away from him, he tightened his hold.

"Nope, don't look at me like that."

"Like what?"

"I didn't mean I don't want you like that." He sighed and set his forehead against hers. "I meant that I wanted to take my time."

"I will point out, once again, that we haven't just met."

"But…" Then he trailed off. She waited for what seemed like hours, even as she knew only a few seconds had passed before he continued. "You matter."

She blinked against the sudden burning against the backs of her eyes. She hated crying, but no one had said those words in such a growly slash tender way. It seeped into her soul.

"You matter, too," she said in a whisper.

"We should take it slow."

She understood he was repeating a mantra like a rule as if he was reminding himself to take it slow. At that moment, she decided to push him. There was no reason not to act on this need, this heat that was simmering between them.

She slid her hand down his chest. "We *have* been taking it slow."

He opened his mouth, but nothing came out. Probably because she pressed her hand against a very impressive length. She wanted to feel that inside her, and she needed it like yesterday. She wasn't usually so aggressive when it came to men, but she'd been dying to touch him for months, and now that she had, she wanted it all.

He closed his eyes for a second and when he opened them, the dark need Eileen witnessed had her stomach muscles quivering. She could admit to herself that it scared her a little, but at the same time, she knew she wanted it. Her entire body throbbed with the desire to taste.

"You're sure?"

She nodded. "I've never been so sure of anything in my life."

Declan swooped in and took complete possession of her mouth. The simmering heat went to boiling in mere seconds. No man had ever been able to do that to her, make her forget everything but him. She had always thought women were lying when they talked about how men could do that to them. Apparently, she had been kissing the wrong guys.

His tongue slipped between her lips. Her nipples hardened at that little move. He was so damned talented with his tongue that she was ready to lose it right then. To rub herself against him like a cat.

All of a sudden, his mouth was gone. It was so abrupt she was blinking, but in the next instant, he grabbed her hand and dragged her back to his bedroom. Like the rest of the apartment, the room had a light, airy feel, with a massive king-sized bed in the middle.

He faced her. "Last chance, love. You have a chance to run before I get my mitts on you."

She looked at him. He was every fantasy she had about any man. Tall, strong, sexy as hell, with a mouth that could seduce her. Yes, they had cussed, but he had barely touched her, and she could feel her damn panties. Something was coursing through her with the arousal: fear. It licked around the outskirts, and she knew there was a good chance she should listen to what that one part of her was saying. But...it was drowned out by the need surging through her.

With careful movements, she stepped back and saw his disappointment. Then, she grabbed the bottom of her shirt and tugged it over her head, tossing it behind her.

One slow blink, then he stepped forward. "I guess that's a yes.

He laughed. It sent sparks of energy through her entire body, but it also had her heart turning over. Without much effort, he picked her up and tossed her onto the bed. She laughed. When had she last done that with a man? She couldn't remember.

"I like that sound," he said before tugging his shirt off. When he stepped out of his jeans, she was saddened to see that he was wearing boxer briefs. She was sure he was a guy that would go commando. Still, it was easy to see his hard length outlined by the soft black fabric.

"What's that sad look for, baby?"

She hated when guys used the word *baby*. Or at least, she had before Declan had said it. Now, she wanted to hear him say it all the time.

"I thought you wouldn't have anything on under those jeans."

He laughed at that. "I need to keep it in check tonight. I swore I would take this slowly, but we are going all in since you insisted."

Leaning down, he helped tug off her jeans. They joined the rest of the clothes on the floor. Then, he was crawling on the bed, covering her body with his. He gave her a long, wet kiss, pulling her bottom lip between his teeth, teasing her before he kissed down her neck. With expert ease, he undid her bra and had her panties off before she could even think twice.

Then, he was between her legs. He kissed her inner thigh, nipping at the sensitive skin. Next, he was moving up, dragging the flat of his tongue along the way.

"I've been dying to know what you tasted like from the first time I saw you."

After that, his mouth was on her sex. Every nerve ending was tingling, so aware of the sensual torture, ready to explode. She needed this, needed him. His tongue slipped inside of her, tasting the most intimate part of her. She rarely enjoyed having a man go down on her, but she thought it had to do with trust... and technique. Declan Fitzpatrick was a sex god.

"Fucking delicious. You taste better than any fantasy I could ever have."

He slipped a finger inside of her as he teased her clit with his tongue, then his teeth. Her fingers speared through all that thick hair as her toes curled into the mattress. She was so close, but it seemed out of reach.

"Come on, baby. Let me feel you come all over my fingers."

That was all it took. She was flying high over that last hurdle to break apart into a million pieces. Her orgasm seemed to last forever, her body shuddering as she bucked up against his mouth. All the way, he continued to lick, nip, and tease. Before she knew what was happening, she was up and over into another orgasm.

Soon, he slipped up her body, licking and sucking and nipping. The man seemed to be treating her like a delicacy. And she did not mind it at all. In fact, Eileen didn't know if she had ever felt so sexy and powerful in her life.

Declan reached over to his nightstand to grab a condom. With fast moves, he tugged off his boxers. His cock sprang free, and Eileen couldn't help herself. She reached forward, wrapped her hand around his thick length, and stroked him from the tip down to the base.

"Damn," Declan muttered, his voice hoarse with need. A drop of precum wet the head. She licked her lips, thinking about how he would taste.

"Nope, not this time. You do that, and I will go off like a rocket, and while I wouldn't mind getting off that way next time, this time, I want to be deep inside of you when I come."

After easing her down, he tore open the condom package, pulled it out, and then rolled it down his shaft. He lifted her by her hips and centered his tip at her entrance. In one fast, hard thrust, he was inside of her. She was sensitive from her release, but she soon adjusted.

"Oh, fuck, Eileen, you feel good wrapped around me, baby."

He started to move, each thrust measured. She wasn't the kind of woman who had multiple orgasms, but soon, she felt the tension building. His fingers dug into her hips as he increased his speed.

"Pinch your nipples, Eileen."

Again, it was totally out of character for her, but she did as he ordered. He groaned. She opened her eyes and looked up at him. He was watching her with hooded eyes as he licked his lips. It was like he was remembering what she tasted like.

"Come for me, Eileen. I want to feel you coming all over my dick."

He pressed his thumb against her clit, and it was her undoing. One...two...on the third thrust, she was losing it again, screaming his name as her orgasm slammed into her more brutal than the first. That seemed to be all he needed.

"Fuck, yes, Eileen," he muttered.

He sped up his rhythm, thrusting so hard and so deep that the bed slammed against the wall. He threw his head back and shouted her name as he lost himself to the pleasure.

He collapsed on top of her a moment later, but she didn't care. He was heavy, but she enjoyed his weight on her. He stirred a few moments later and then lifted his head.

"I'm sorry I dropped on you like an oaf."

She chuckled and squeezed her arms around him. "I don't mind."

He kissed her, his mouth moving over hers lightly, seductive. "Be right back."

Nodding, she let him go as she tried to get her head screwed on straight. That had been...well, the best sex of her life. She knew it was probably normal for him, but she understood that she trusted him on some level to let herself go like that.

"I need some water, you?"

"Please."

He didn't take long to return with two glasses of water and her phone. "I thought you would need this nearby."

"Thanks," she said, setting it on the bedside table. "So, you don't mind having me stay the night?"

"No," he said, then his lips curved as he looked at her. He was still completely naked. "I'm not done with ya."

"Is that a fact?"

He nodded, then said, "Why don't I show you?"

Eileen was laughing when he dove back on the bed.

Nine

Buzzing woke Declan. It wasn't uncommon for his irritating family to wake him up with phone calls or texts. What was unusual was the warm woman next to him.

Eileen.

She had been more than anything he could have imagined. He had taken her another two times during the night. No. He had taken her once, and then she had taken him. Equal. He smiled at that.

The buzzing stopped. He pulled Eileen closer, enjoying her clean feminine scent. For a woman who spent her days in the darkest muck Baltimore had to offer, she reminded him of clean spring breezes.

He was just drifting back to sleep when the buzzing started again. He was going to kill whoever it was, especially when Eileen stirred against him.

Declan grabbed his phone from his nightstand and realized it wasn't his that was buzzing.

"Is that mine?"

"Yeah, love, it is."

She sighed and opened her eyes. The flutter of her lashes... then those brilliant eyes. God, he would never get used to seeing those. He knew one thing: he would like to see her wake up every damned morning for the rest of his life.

He blinked. What the hell? Why was he thinking like that? Because she's important. She had been since the moment he'd met her. That had to be why he took his time before asking her out.

With considerable effort—and a little grumbling that he found cute—she reached over to grab her phone.

"O'Reilly."

Then she was silent as she listened to whoever was on the phone. Declan decided it was the perfect time to lean forward and kiss her shoulder. She shivered and glanced back at him.

"Get bent, Eddie. It's the middle of the night. I was sleeping."

She was silent as she listened to her partner talk, but he knew something bad had happened. Of course, it did. It was before three in the morning, and she was a homicide detective. Pretty sure it was a bad sign when your partner called you under those circumstances.

He watched as the warmth in her gaze dissolved into cold, hard detective eyes. It was...well, a little scary, but also hot as fuck. This woman was a bundle of contradictions that kept him on his toes. All sides of her personality called to him, from the sweet woman who laughed at his stories and praised his food to the vixen who drove him insane last night to the hard-edged detective.

He wanted it all.

"Okay, I'll meet you there."

She clicked her phone off and sighed. He could feel the tension vibrating through her body.

"I gotta go."

"I figured."

She glanced back at him once more. "Sorry."

He shook his head. "Don't be. It's your job."

She sighed. "I really would rather be in bed with you."

It sounded like a confession.

"I would like that too. Do you have time for a shower?"

"Do you mind?"

He smiled. "No. I was hoping for a shower together this morning, but I'll take a rain check." Surprise lit her features, and he frowned. "What?"

"So you want a repeat?"

He snorted. "Woman, I'm not even close to being done with you."

Declan was starting to think he never would be. The sweet smile Eileen gave him went straight to his heart. Leaning down, she cupped his face and brushed her mouth against his. He wanted more. To taste, to take. But he knew she had work to do, so he forced himself to take what she could give him. As she pulled away, her sigh of longing filled the room.

"Take your shower, and I'll put on some coffee."

He watched as she slipped from his bed and walked into the bathroom without an ounce of embarrassment. That ass. He closed his eyes briefly and then forced himself out of bed. After throwing on a pair of sweatpants and a T-shirt, he hurried to the kitchen. He wanted to ensure she had something to eat before she left, so he grabbed the bread he'd made yesterday and tossed it in the toaster. After that, he went to work on the coffee. By the time she walked out ten minutes later, she looked fresh and sexy, and he had a container of food ready for her.

"You use cream, right?"

"Yeah. How do you know that?"

"The brunch my mother had."

It was four months ago, but he was starting to think there wouldn't be much about this woman that he didn't remember.

He had the coffee in a to-go cup from his restaurant. She took it and sipped it, her eyes lighting up. "Perfect."

"Here," he said, handing her a bag. She frowned and looked inside.

"You made me breakfast."

"Hardly what I planned."

One eyebrow rose. "You planned breakfast? Like you expected to get lucky?"

His face heated. "No. It was last night. After."

"After? Like after you blew my mind with hot monkey sex, you planned breakfast?"

Her teasing tone had him blushing again. Like he was some teenager and not a man in his early thirties. "Don't we have to get going? You have a crime scene, right?"

She sighed, and he hated it when her smile faded. "Yeah. I'll get a ride-share."

"Absolutely not. I'll take you."

"Declan."

"No. My mother taught me right."

"So, again, after the hot monkey sex, she told you to take your bed partner to a crime scene?"

He grabbed his keys and stepped around the island. This close, he could smell his soap on her and that unique scent. "No. She told me every lady should be treated with respect."

Her eyes softened.

"Plus, you can eat while I drive."

"Which I could do in a ride share. Damn." She sighed. "I don't have my gun."

"Do I need to drop you off at home?"

She shook her head. "I'll have Eddie drop me off after we work the scene. That way, I can throw on some work clothes."

"Do you want some guacamole with your toast?"

"That would be fabulous."

He grabbed one of the small containers out of the fridge that he'd made up the day before and handed it to her.

"Come on. Let's go."

There was something almost normal about this moment. It was like they had been doing this for decades. And Declan found that he didn't mind it one bit.

BY THE TIME they reached the crime scene, Eileen had polished off the toast. The man was a god of good food. It was just before dawn, so the crime scene was illuminated by lights set up by the police. Another alley not too far from Fleet Street.

"Thanks for bringing me. And for breakfast and dinner. And for the hot monkey sex."

His face flushed again, and she fought a giggle. She shouldn't find joy like this at a crime scene, but there was something so wonderful about making Declan blush. The man had a dirty mouth in bed, and he knew just how to make a woman come multiple times, but he blushed when she teased him. It was so delicious.

"I'd like to do it all again," he said.

"Which part?"

He stared into her eyes, solemn, especially for Declan, and filled with intensity. "All of it."

Her heart turned over at his tone. God, the man made her head spin with just three words.

"I would like that too."

"I assume you'll have a long day."

She nodded and waited. This is where guys got a little pushy. Maybe not right off the bat, but she had trigger words. Things like: Pretty women shouldn't want to hang out with dead bodies. Those words always got to her.

"Don't forget to eat."

When he said nothing else, she nodded and leaned across the console. She needed one more taste before she went to deal with the horror of another murder.

"I'll text you," she said.

He nodded. Then, she slipped out of the car and headed to the crime scene. She could feel his attention on her, watching as if he wanted to ensure she made it to the crime scene without incident. It was stupid because she could handle herself, but it warmed her heart. Men didn't tend to take care of her.

Once she reached the tape, she glanced back and waved. It was then that he pulled away and headed back to his place.

"Oh, my, I don't think I've ever heard of this happening," her cousin Ritchie said. God, she couldn't get away from the O'Reillys.

"Murders happen every day, Richard."

"No. I don't think anyone would ever say you were known to do the walk of shame."

True. She rarely stayed over at her lovers' homes. And if she had them at her house, she would suggest they leave. Eileen wasn't a snuggler, although last night proved her wrong. She hadn't wanted to leave Declan's place unless he was going with her.

"Wonder what Zane and Zac would say about it?"

"About as much as Margie would say about you slobbering all over Fiona."

Oh, yeah. She loved Ritchie, but he couldn't keep it in his pants. He'd been dating Margie for about three years, and she knew what he was like. She would believe Eileen if she came in and told her about him cheating.

"You play tough."

"Don't forget it."

Then she headed off to Eddie, who was standing at the mouth of the alley. Pushing aside the humor and the warm fuzzies left over from her night with Declan, she rolled her shoulders.

"So, like the other one?"

He glanced at her, then his gaze went down, taking in her clothes. With a glance in the direction from where she came, his lips curved. "Good for you, O'Reilly."

"Cut it out. Already got shit from Ritchie, who threatened to say something to Zac and Zane."

"Uh, you're a woman in her thirties. Maybe they shouldn't care."

They wouldn't. They knew she could handle herself. The only time they seemed to step in was with Bryan.

"But, yes, it's like the other night. Down to the ornate handle on the knife."

"Dark hair?"

He nodded. "Stripped of her clothes, but I bet we get no

DNA, especially if there isn't any sexual assault. She's also not as athletic. More...too thin."

She glanced at him. "Maybe a sex worker?"

"Maybe."

"So, the first one was a date, which is irritating because we still don't have a lead on that."

"Yeah."

That one word dripped with frustration. Eileen understood the feeling. They'd even had a uniform spend long hours reviewing security feeds from Fitzpatrick's and the surrounding areas. The guy never showed up on those. There was someone with Irene, but it was like the guy knew where the cameras were. His back was always to the lens.

"If she was a sex worker, there's a better chance we'll identify her fast," he said. She nodded.

"I'll check in with Sharlene."

"Go ahead. Then you can tell me about your date."

She rolled her eyes and headed off to the alley. Eddie was worse than a teenager when it came to gossip, although she knew he kept anything they talked about close to his chest. It was why she'd jumped at the chance to pair off with him when her old partner had retired.

"Well, look at you," Sharlene said. These people. "Second time in a month, you look like you have a life. What is going on with you?"

"People show up to scenes all the time in various stages of dress. Why is everyone so interested in the way I'm dressed?"

"Because this is you. You never show up like this. Was that a Fitzpatrick I saw dropping you off?"

"Declan."

"Smart choice. Get the one who cooks. Although, I've

found a lot of firehouse folks know how to cook—in more ways than in the kitchen."

Eileen smiled, but it faded. "So, our vic?"

"She was out here for a little bit. Like the other night, rain washed away some of the evidence, but that knife... looks almost identical. Like it's part of a set."

"Hopefully, with just two."

"Do you ever get that lucky?"

She shook her head. "She does look underweight."

"Yeah. Maybe a sex worker, but she could have just been a drug user."

That caught her attention. The last vic had been an upstanding member of society. She barely drank, from what her friends said. In fact, the mystery man was out of character for her. Since the mess of her last relationship, she hadn't dated. Now, a possible drug user and/or sex worker?

"Drug user?"

"Nothing on the arms, but, looking between the toes, she was shooting up."

"Which means she might have been trying to hide it?"

The ME nodded. A lot of IV drug users shot up between their toes to hide the fact that they were using.

"She was out here longer, but it was a Monday night. Not as much foot traffic."

"TOD?"

"I would say five hours or less."

Eileen drew in a deep breath. It was just now, just after five in the morning.

"Good to know. Hopefully, we can get some help from the cameras."

"Fingers crossed. I'll do a tox screen, of course. I'll text you when I'm done."

Eileen wasn't one for standing around while the ME worked. There was no reason to hover when she was doing her work. It didn't make the investigation go any faster, and she could have spent her time running down leads.

She walked back to Eddie, ignoring the puddles since she was wearing boots. "TOD is about five hours ago."

"And another rainy night."

She sighed. "I hope that isn't this guy's trigger because we're moving into a very rainy month."

April could be insanely wet for Baltimore.

"Yeah. Do you want me to drop you at home so you can change?"

"Mainly, so I can get my gun. I feel naked."

Eddie made a face. "Don't. It would be like seeing my sister naked."

She smiled. "Let's go so we can get in there and start reviewing footage."

The moment they stepped closer to the tape, Eileen realized they had attracted the news. That was normal, but this hit right at early morning rush hour...

"How was she found?"

"Anonymous tip."

"Dammit." It had been perfectly timed to garner attention from the early morning news in Baltimore and DC.

"What?"

"Timing."

Understanding lit his expression. "I can't wait to find this asshole. He needs to be taken down."

She slipped under the tape. "The Baltimore PD has no comment at this time."

Questions were thrown in her direction, but one caught her attention. "Is this the same as Irene's murder?"

She ignored it because she wouldn't give the vulture anything to feed off of, but it struck down in her soul. When they slipped into Eddie's car, she took note of one reporter, who continued to stand there and watch them.

Arnie Matthews. The guy was always after sensationalist crap to get more views and clicks.

No one else had made that connection. She would definitely be looking into Arnie, because she didn't need people making the connections right now. It could hinder the investigation.

And just like her partner, she couldn't wait to find the asshole and lock him in a dark hole.

HE WATCHED FROM THE SHADOWS. Rain had started again, but he didn't care and knew he wouldn't be noticed. He blended in with these people. Most of them wouldn't look at him twice.

Eileen said something to the reporter and walked away. He had seen her show up with that man. The bastard thought he had a right to her, but he would soon learn that Eileen wasn't for him. Why would she want someone who cooked for a living? Not when she could have a man who was helping her career. She was getting attention for the case, and when they realized they had the same killer, she would get more news.

It was only a matter of time before she realized she was meant for him.

Ten

Declan smiled when his sister walked into his restaurant. They weren't open yet, but he had called her down because he needed help. She had little Mike with her, so that made him happy.

"Come here, big guy," he said, easily taking his nephew.

"Tell me why I had to run over here on my day off."

He sighed.

"Tell me you didn't screw up your date last night."

"How did you know about that?"

"Really? This family is only outdone in gossiping by the Santinis. Please tell me you didn't screw up."

"No," he said, grabbing a fresh towel to wipe off Mike's drool. The boy was teething like crazy.

"Okay, why do you need me? And why couldn't we do this over the phone?"

"First, I feel better talking this over in person. And second, I took BeeBee's advice and took Eileen food one night. And since I cooked for her last night—" One eyebrow rose, and, at that moment, he saw his mother. He knew that he couldn't lie to Kaitlin. "But when she had to leave this morning, I couldn't do more than coffee and avocado toast."

She blinked. "One date, and you got her to sleep over?"

Something in his sister's voice had him tilting his head to study her. "Yeah. Why?"

She pressed her lips together as if trying to keep a secret.

"Really? Now? You're gonna not tell me something I need to know?"

"You might need to know, but I'm trying to remember if it was told to me in confidence or not."

"For the love of —"

"Okay, here, I can do this." She drew in a deep breath, and he called on his control not to yell at her. Not because he wouldn't yell at her. It was because little Mike was watching them. Declan would not lose his temper in front of the little man. "Say I have this friend."

"Jesus, Mary, and Joseph," he muttered. For some reason, Mike found that hilarious. "I don't want to meet any friend of yours."

She settled her hands on her hips and stared at him as if he were stupid. Then, it hit him what she was doing. See, that's the thing. Before his infatuation with Eileen, he would have picked up on it. When Aeden had once told him that love made a man stupid—in good ways and bad—his brother hadn't been lying.

"Go on."

"This friend made a comment one night. We were talking about sleeping with a significant other."

"I don't want to hear about you and your sleeping partner. Gross."

An eye roll. "This was after I was married. I didn't know the friend before that."

"Oh, yeah." See. He knew she had been assigned Wendy's case earlier that year, and that's how she had shown up in his orbit.

"Anyway, I was saying it was nice to snuggle with Brando."

"Gross. But go on."

"This friend said that Eileen didn't like spending the night or having a guy spend the night. She actually said she wasn't a cuddler."

Everything seemed to stop around him. Or he didn't notice much else other than those words. Wasn't a cuddler? He had pulled her close and kept her that way all night long. She hadn't protested or even suggested that he take her home. He remembered her sigh of contentment as she settled on his chest the night before.

"I take it Eileen spent the entire night?"

"Well, until she got called to a scene."

Her eyes widened. "And?"

He shrugged. "I drove her there."

His sister's lips twitched. "So, why am I here?"

"I need some advice and wanted to talk to you in person."

"And? Jeez, Declan, just spit it out."

"That Sunday after the party, I took her dinner. Then I cooked her dinner."

"And breakfast."

"Hardly cooking. Toast with a mashed-up avocado."

"Believe me, that's big. When I was with that idiot I was engaged to, he never did things like that. But Brando does things like that all the time. It's amazing."

"So, if I sent her lunch, you don't think that would be too much?"

There was a beat of silence. "Oh...ohhhhh. Declan."

There was excitement in her voice.

"What?"

She shook her head. "Nothing. Listen, she would probably appreciate it. More, send her partner something too."

"I don't know what he likes."

Mike was playing with his hair, which he had yet to put up.

"Let me think. Eileen said they came in and ate one day, and you weren't here. It was the day all you losers went fishing."

"Love you too, sis." Sarcasm was easy to hear in his voice. He didn't even try to hide it.

"Be nice. I'm trying to help you."

"Sorry."

"Okay. She said she had your shepherd's pie—because that's her go-to. Although I know she loves Italian food. So keep that in mind."

"I made Italian last night. I remembered you mentioning it."

"But her partner had your mushroom and Swiss burger. He apparently raved about it for a week afterward."

"I already took her Shepard's pie once a couple weeks ago."

"She also adores your clam chowder with the ham sandwich thing. She mentioned that."

He frowned. "Does Eileen talk a lot about food?"

"Maybe. It's because Eileen can't cook."

"Just because she has a time-consuming job doesn't mean she can't cook."

"No, as in boiling water is hard for her. She just hates it, too."

Hates cooking? What the hell?

"Hey, don't look so upset. I think it's perfect."

"That she doesn't cook?"

One of his greatest joys was working in the kitchen. Being with someone who hated cooking... would be a first.

"Listen to your big sister," she said, drawing his attention back to her. "Every relationship is about things you can share, but it is also about that yin/yang thing. You know Brando and I are really different."

"You're both nerds."

She cocked her head to the side in warning. His mouth was going to get in him so much trouble.

"We are different in other ways as well. Because of that military upbringing and him being in the military, he plans out every danged thing. I get having plans, but do I know what I want to do three weeks from now for dinner? No. But I bet Brando does. So, he keeps me on track for the important things."

"That sounds like a nightmare."

"On the other hand," she said, ignoring his comment, "I help him be more spontaneous. Your differences should make you a stronger couple. If it doesn't, then it won't last."

"We aren't a couple."

But you want to be.

God, that thought had him almost dropping his nephew.

"What the hell is *that* look for?"

"Should you be cussing in front of your son?"

"Did it bother you to cook for her last night?" Kaitlin asked as she motioned for him to give her Mike. With regret, he handed his nephew over.

"No."

He liked it. He always wanted to cook for people, but something was different last night. Really, every time he was cooking for her or even plating up food for her, there was this feeling of how important her well-being was to him. He wanted to take care of her...needed to take care of her.

Oh, damn.

He might be in a lot of trouble, like in love kind of trouble.

"What's that look for?"

He blinked, trying to push back his panic. What if it wasn't reciprocated? He did not like that idea. Still, he knew he was helpless to avoid it...her.

"Nothing. Just, you think I should send her lunch?"

"What time did you feed her?"

"Before five."

She nodded. "Send her lunch. Normally, she only has chips or a candy bar for lunch. I have to get going. Ma and I are hanging out today."

He leaned over the bar and kissed his sister on the cheek. "Thanks."

"No worries. Only, just be sure about Eileen. I like the two of you together. She needs someone to take care of her."

"She can take care of herself."

"Oh, I know she can. But having someone to take care of you, not because they want something in return, now that is fantastic. And, Declan, you need someone to take care of. Just be careful. Her job is high-powered, and I know there is talk of moving her up in the ranks. I know she wants that. It means a more public image, and you have to be sure you want that."

Like that would scare him away. He saw the two of them out, then locked up as he started to plan. He knew he seemed obsessed with food, and that was what had led him to be a chef. Now, though, he seemed to be obsessed with feeding Eileen.

By NOON, almost every news organization in the DMV—the DC, Maryland, and Virginia—area had jumped on the Arnie bandwagon. It was only a matter of time before the national news picked it up. It could blow their case up, and Eileen wasn't in the mood for the press or their insanity.

"O'Reilly. Francisco. My office," Captain Mathers said. They followed him into his office. Mathers was a demanding boss, but he was solid. The older African American had served in the Army before donning the same uniform his father and brothers wore. Another legacy.

"Thanks for the heads-up earlier," he said as he sat behind his desk. Both she and Eddie took a seat. "I told them no, but is there a connection?"

She shrugged. "We have nothing to link the murders except the knife and where they were found."

"That could be enough."

"It could be," Eddie said. "Could be a copycat, although we have kept some things out of the news. The knife in particular."

"Don't get me wrong. You're my best two detectives. I just need this cleared and soon. I do not need this city going to shit because of tabloid reporting."

"Noted," she murmured. "We're going through CCTV and running searches on the knives. ME has sent it to forensics, but I want to see if the designs are similar."

"That sounds like a good start. The first one had a boyfriend you were looking at?"

"He was in jail the night of Irene's murder," Eddie said. "Drunken brawl."

Mathers sighed. "That sucks. Any other leads?"

"Still looking for the guy she was dating," Eileen said."

He nodded, and then he glanced at Eddie. "Can you give us a minute?"

Her partner looked at her, then back at their captain. "Sure." He headed out of the office, shutting the door behind him.

"You two seem to be working out well."

She nodded. "Eddie is fantastic."

"So, why do you want to leave?"

She frowned. "What? I never said I wanted to leave."

"You don't have to lie to me, Eileen. I've known you since you were a senior in high school."

He had. Her father and the captain had been acquaintances. "I'm not lying. I worked too hard to get homicide. Truth is, have my eye on your job when you retire."

His smile came and went. "I hoped those were your thoughts because you would make an excellent captain."

Warmth filled her chest. The captain wasn't a man who threw out compliments. You had to earn those, and him saying that to her made her day.

"So, why so serious?" Then something horrible hit her. "You aren't sick, are you?"

His eyes widened. "No. Nothing like that. I know that this job isn't easy, especially as a woman. For me, as a black man, it was hard, but it will be even worse for a woman. It's a drain on you and your family."

She rolled her eyes. "Yeah, well, the O'Reillys have been serving as long as there has been a police department."

"I'm talking about if you should want to get married. Have kids."

Declan flashed through her mind for some reason, but she pushed that aside. She couldn't get distracted by that man or what his talented hands could do. Especially while she was discussing things with the captain.

"Oh."

"Yeah, oh. I just think you need to understand what will be expected of them. This job almost split Mary and me."

Surprise hit her hard. Mary was the captain's wife. Sweet, funny, and dedicated to her family, she taught psychology at one of the local universities.

"I see you had no idea, and I'm glad. It wasn't too long after I was picked for captain here. I had to prove myself." He shook his head as his gaze moved over to a framed pic on his desk. She knew it was Mary and their two boys. Then, his attention shifted back to Eileen. "Make sure they know the score if you get seriously involved with someone. This case has a chance to make a name for you and Eddie. You are the lead. Remember that. But also remember the press might start looking into you. Following you because they are sure if they harass you, they will get you to spill your secrets."

Eileen shook her head. "That's never going to happen."

"I know that, but it won't stop the press if this case goes sideways."

She nodded.

"I thought that's why you wanted to leave."

"Because I had a date last night?" Who drove her to the crime scene this morning. That was abnormal but it wasn't a problem for most other people.

"You did?" He shook his head. "I'm not talking about that. I'm talking about how you're gonna work for your brothers."

"Wait. What?"

His eyes narrowed as he studied her. "There's a rumor going through the precinct that you're planning on jumping ship."

"To work for Zac and Zane?"

He nodded.

"No. Never in a million years. I do not want to deal with those nut jobs. Or the jobs they take." She rolled her eyes. "They do some investigating, mainly protection or security assessments. Also, I would rather work security at a mall before I worked for them. Who would think I'd want to work for them?"

His mouth twitched. "Those were a lot of words."

She felt her cheeks burning. "Sorry, but no. I like to be here, working for everyone."

"Okay. Well, someone is spreading the rumor."

"It's not me, and I'll check in with the two of them. I do not want to leave, and they have never suggested it."

He sighed, relief easy to hear. "Good. Now, get back out there and find out who is killing women. I would hate it if the FBI came in on this one."

She nodded and headed out. Eileen stood just outside of his door and looked over the precinct. Who the hell was telling people that she wanted to leave?

That's when she noticed one of the servers from Declan's restaurant standing by her desk. She knew the young woman was working through college by waiting tables. Did she have anything she needed to tell them about the case?

Excitement lit through her as she stepped toward her desk,

only to have her way blocked by Bryan. Ugh, this was getting to be a problem.

"Captain Mathers seemed like he had something to talk to you about.

Why had she been attracted to this idiot? Yes, she had been young, but she had not been stupid. Maybe a little naive, but it went beyond that. She had been thankful that she had never slept with him. He had been pressuring her, but she knew it would be a mistake to do that at the academy. Whether fair or not, that would have given her a reputation.

"Yes. It was about the cases."

"Don't you mean case?"

Her eyes narrowed as she studied him. She was tired of his bullshit, and she was hungry. That avocado toast Declan had made her had only gone so far. Her stomach had been growling for an hour.

Then it hit her that Bryan always heard gossip first. "Have you heard anyone say I wanted to leave the precinct?"

He shook his head. "Who would believe that? Your entire life is wrapped up in your work here."

The bitterness she heard almost had her taking a step back. Instead, she nodded. "Let me know if you hear anything. That's a server from Fitzpatrick's, so I need to see if she has any information for me."

She stepped around him and headed to her desk. "Hey, Fee."

Fiona Markle was her name, but she went by Fee. "Did you have something you wanted to add to your statement?"

Her eyes widened, then she shook her head. "No. The boss sent you lunch. Well, for you and your partner."

She glanced at Eddie, who was plowing through a hamburger.

"Sorry that I kept you waiting."

The younger woman shook her head. "Don't worry. Slow day, and the boss always pays well when we deliver to friends and family."

Still, she grabbed her purse and pulled out a ten. Fee shook her head. "Boss said not to take a tip."

She rolled her eyes. "Then take it, and we'll keep it between us. Thanks for delivering the food."

The waitress smiled and slipped the ten in her back pocket. "No problem."

With that, she walked away.

"If this gets us free lunch, I am all for you sleeping with Fitzpatrick."

She frowned at her partner. "Why don't you just put up a big neon sign about my sex life?"

"You want me to do that? Neon is really expensive these days."

She sighed and dropped down into her chair. "I just like to keep my personal life separate. Also, you know how men are around here."

"Well, they can get bent. You're a grown-ass woman with a sex life. Idiots."

She smiled at him. "Thanks."

"What did he send you?"

She opened up the cup container and smiled. "Clam chowder and I bet this is a baguette ham and cheese sandwich."

Before she could start eating, though, she had to thank the man.

Eileen: *Thanks for lunch.*

"Tell him thanks from me. Also, I will trade secrets about you for a burger any day of the week."

She flipped him off, and he just laughed.

Declan: *You are most welcome. How is it?*

Like he had to ask.

Eileen: *Haven't started yet. I was in with the captain.*

Declan: *I order you to eat.*

Eileen: *Oh, do you, now? Also, Eddie said he would trade secrets for a burger any day of the week.*

Three dots appeared, then disappeared. Then reappeared before the text came in.

Declan: *I might have to take him up on that. Now, stop texting with me and eat.*

So, for once in her life, she would do what a man told her to and start eating. God, the man knew how to cook, and before long, she had devoured the whole thing.

"Damn, that was fast," Eddie said.

"Like you can talk."

He smiled at her just as her phone rang. She thought it was going to be Declan, but she was wrong. Instead, it was a reporter she knew worked for one of the big national news agencies. She sighed. Since she was the lead on the case, she couldn't ignore him.

"O'Reilly."

"Detective O'Reilly, this is Johnathon Carmichael, and I understand you have a serial in town."

"We do?"

There was a pause. "I thought there had been a connection made between the two cases in the last two weeks. Young women stabbed to death with a knife with an ornate handle."

That had not been released to the public.

"We have not made any connections between the two cases." It was true. The two women did not cross paths that they could tell. "And even so, you know that the FBI considers serials to be three or more murders that are similar."

"Hmm. That's odd. I had Detective Henry call me with the information."

For a long moment, she didn't say anything. Vic Henry died ten years earlier. She knew because he had been one of the detectives who had worked on the Norma Wilson case.

"From this precinct? I think you've had a prank caller. We don't have a Detective Henry here."

Another long pause. She wasn't lying since they genuinely didn't have a Henry there anymore.

"If you could give us the number, we could run it down for you."

"It was an unknown caller."

"Ah, well, sorry about that. I don't know who would be messing with you."

"If I could get a comment from you?"

"No comment. Johnathon, you know we do not make statements about ongoing investigations."

"Fine. I will find this person."

"You do that."

She hung up. "Who was that?" Eddie asked.

"Johnathon Carmichael."

Then, she rose out of her seat and headed back to the captain's office. She knocked and waited for him to call her in.

"Didn't you just leave here?"

She rolled her eyes. "Johnathon Carmichael has someone feeding him BS stories."

"Are they BS stories?"

She sighed. "Not sure. The problem is that the guy is using the name Detective Henry."

The captain's eyes narrowed, and she knew he understood the implications. It could be a coincidence, but seeing how Norma Wilson was stabbed to death and the former Detective Henry was one of the guys on the case, the caller had linked the cold case and their new case. That could mean they have a copycat.

"Damn."

"Exactly."

Eleven

B y seven that night, Declan was antsy. It was an odd feeling for him. He usually loved hanging out in his restaurant and truly enjoyed his work. It wasn't like there weren't bad nights or even bad employees. But most of the time, he was happy at work.

Tonight was different. Tonight, Declan would rather be with Eileen. Even thinking her name had his dick twitching. The women already tugged at him on a level he wasn't sure he liked.

"What is up with you?" Seamus asked as he studied Declan. Out of all of them, Seamus was good at rooting out that something was off with one of them.

"Nothing."

His brother locked his gaze on Declan as he took a long drink from his beer.

"Stop that. It doesn't work."

He smiled because even to Declan's own ears, he sounded defensive.

"Fine. I sent Eileen lunch. I haven't heard from her."

There was a long beat of silence.

"And her partner. I made sure Eddie had something to eat, too."

Seamus's eyes widened. "Wooing her with food?"

"No." Then, "Okay, maybe. She seems to like it when I cook for her."

"Everyone likes it when you cook for them."

"No. That Cindy did not like my food."

His brother snorted. "Cindy didn't like any food. Why you dated a model, I have no idea."

Madness in the form of Eileen O'Reilly. Cindy wasn't exactly a model. She was more of an aspiring model with a few local gigs, and while she was nice enough and the sex had been... okay, she had been the antithesis of Eileen. Eileen wasn't short, but she was authentic. And she loved to eat. Cindy did not. She wanted to eat as few calories as possible. Nothing wrong with that, but damn, it was complicated to make her a meal.

"Yeah, well, I haven't heard from her. I mean, she thanked me in a text."

"That's good."

"And she tipped the server I sent even though she didn't need to."

"Of course she did. She waited tables when she went to college."

"Yeah, I know that." Wait. "How did you know that?"

"Hmm, might have been Kaitlin or Wendy who mentioned it."

He nodded. "She's been at work a long time today."

"She's used to it."

He knew that, but it didn't make him like it anymore. He had always been someone who liked to comfort friends and family. Most of the time, it was with food, but now, he wanted to care for Eileen.

"Hey, they're talking about Irene," Sandy said. Declan turned to face the TV closest to him.

"There are sources inside the Baltimore PD that say the two murders could be linked."

Then, there was a scene outside of Eileen's precinct. She and Eddie were walking out together, and they were stopped by the camera.

"Detective O'Reilly, do you have a comment about the two cases being linked?"

"No comment, just like I told you earlier."

She brushed past him, but the reporter wasn't giving up.

"Don't you think the women of Baltimore deserve an answer?"

That stopped her, and when she turned around to face the reporter, irritation sizzled in her eyes.

"Oh, damn, that guy is never going to get an interview with Eileen," Seamus murmured.

Declan curled his fingers to make fists. Fuck, he hated anyone saying things like that about Eileen. She cared so much about her job, and this asshole was making it sound like she was hiding things. Other people might not see how tired she was, but he did. He also was up close and personal with just how little sleep she'd had last night. Guilt hit him when he realized he had kept her up when she should have been resting. Not that he would change anything about last night, but he knew she had to be exhausted.

"I care deeply about the people—men, women, and children—in this city. But linking two murders before we have the entire picture could screw up the investigation, *Johnathon*."

Oh, damn, that tone. That was sexy as hell. Her voice shook with passion and just a little anger. He was pretty sure that most people watching would be on her side.

"So, once again, I will say no comment. When we have more information, then we will let the public know. But there is one thing I have to say." Her gaze focused on the camera and not the reporter. "No matter if it was one or two different men, we *will* catch the perpetrators. A man who would do this is weak. In any other case, a woman could take him down. That's why he does it at night. That's what cowards do."

She turned and headed down the steps with her partner.

"Your woman doesn't take shit off anyone," Seamus said, admiration filling his voice.

His brother might not understand just what happened, but Declan did. Ice careened through his blood as he stared at the TV. Some commercial was playing, but he barely paid attention to it. Seamus was going on about how badass she was, but Declan could barely respond.

Eileen had just put a target on her back, and he was sure she had done it on purpose.

GETTING home seemed to take forever for Eileen. She loved her job, but there were days like today that really tested her abilities. A lot of people thought that cops did their job to go after perps. Granted, that was part of it, but the other part of it was the victims. Today...that had been a hard one to handle.

Eddie had been right. Their victim had been working the streets. Jennifer Rowe was only twenty-three, but she looked older thanks to the life she had led. A runaway at the age of sixteen, she had been homeless for most of those seven years. A heroin addiction had forced her into prostitution. Got to support that habit, right?

Bitterness filled her, and she had to push back on it. It made it difficult to do the job. Relief hit Eileen as she pulled up to the curb in front of her house. Everything seemed to be quiet, thanks to the chilly rain. April was their rainiest month during the Spring, but March could definitely hit them hard because the rain was always so damned cold. Maybe that's why she couldn't get her body to warm up today.

She noticed a package sitting on the stoop as she approached her door. She frowned, trying to remember if she had ordered anything. She picked it up and saw her name, but there was no postmark. There was a good chance Mrs. Kilpatrick had left her some goodies. As cranky as that woman was, she always made Eileen cookies at least once a month. She bent to pick it up, then heard a car drive up and park behind her. Frowning, she turned and noticed it was Declan.

Warmth filled her as she watched him slip out of his truck and walk toward her. That and a little fear. She was so eager to see him, to feel him slip his arms around her and tell her things would be okay, that it scared her. And embarrassed her. Eileen learned early on that men did not do well with her job, and from the irritated look on his face, Declan was angry that she hadn't gotten in touch with him today.

Rude, although she did text her thanks. Part of it was on purpose, and part of it was the job.

It's been one day, and I need him too much.

There were times during the day when she had been irritated or overwhelmed. In those moments, she had wanted

Declan. One freaking date, and he was under her skin. That wasn't good.

"Hey, you okay?"

He was worried about her? She frowned.

"Yeah. Why?"

He shoved his hands into his front pockets. "We—"

"We?"

"Seamus was by the restaurant. We had the news on since it was so slow, and we saw you sticking it to Carmichael."

That had brought her some joy. That asshole had tried to ambush her and Eddie when they left the precinct. Sticking it to him on TV had been worth the annoyed text she got from the captain.

"Yeah, we watched you. I take it you had a tough day?"

She nodded. Eileen knew she shouldn't do it, shouldn't show weakness, but she couldn't help herself. "Wanna come in?"

Relief filled his expression. He had been worried she wouldn't want to spend time with him.

"Only if you feel up to it."

She blinked. Was he leaving the ball in her court? This was new for her.

"But I do need to talk to you."

And there it was.

"Come on."

She unlocked her door, and he followed her into her house. It was warm inside, but she was chilled to the bone. It had nothing to do with the weather but with whatever BS Declan was going to give her. At least he was doing this in person.

It was only one glorious night, and he saw her on TV and realized he wasn't up for it. Some guys would get off on the notoriety. She had already gotten tons of texts from friends and family about it, and she was sure the few unknowns she had ignored came from reporters. It would only get worse before this was over.

She closed the front door, then walked into the kitchen, setting the package down on the counter.

"What do you want to talk about?"

"What's wrong?"

That had her glancing over her shoulder at Declan. He was so big and beautiful, and dammit, she wanted to keep him. She yearned to come home to him, to share her day with him. To just be with him.

Oh, dammit. No, this was wrong. Her dependency wasn't a good thing. All men leave. Her father was different, but she didn't seem to attract the kind of man who wanted to deal with her job. Or her. He had a lot to deal with.

She studied him as panic clawed at her throat. Eileen knew it was a stupid thing to do, but apparently, over the last few months, she had been falling in love with Declan.

What was she going to do about that?

"Now you look sick. Come sit down." She was so stunned by the silent admission that she didn't fight him when he took her by the arm and led her to one of the stools at her counter. He eased her into it.

"I bet you haven't eaten since lunch, have you?"

She shook her head.

He was muttering under his breath as he opened her refrigerator. "How do you survive?"

"Sarcasm and coffee."

Pausing his perusal of her fridge, he sent a narrowed-eye glare over his shoulder. "That is not enough."

"Declan, you said you wanted to talk to me."

He shut the door to the fridge and then faced her. "I didn't like what you did tonight."

"And what was that?"

"You, on camera."

Oh, so he was one of those. There were a lot of guys who liked the cop for the fetish of the whole thing. Then there was the notoriety. Then, some guys didn't like that she had a spotlight. They wanted to be the big man in charge.

"It's part of my job."

"Bullshit."

She blinked. Declan was a rough-and-tumble guy, but she rarely heard him cuss. Well, other than in bed. Then, he had been all down and dirty.

"Are you blushing? Why?"

"Stop changing the subject."

His frown turned darker. "We will come back to that. But I am saying it's bullshit that you had to put a target on your back like that. You practically dared the asshole killing women to come after you."

Her skin iced over. It was precisely what she had been doing. That was why the captain sent her several texts. Oh, and Eddie was furious with her.

Every man—including her brothers—had feelings about what she did.

"No—"

He stepped forward. "Yes, you did. Do you think I don't realize that you look like the women being killed?"

"Similar, just like thousands of other women in this city."

"I don't care about those other women."

"Well, you should."

136

"Well, I don't love them!"

She blinked as her heart boomed in her chest. He looked a little surprised by the comment. "What?"

"Yeah, I didn't want to tell you this way. I have some game, as you saw last night."

"One night, Declan."

He shook his head as he cupped her face in his hands. She felt the calluses on his fingers as he smoothed them over her cheeks. "It's been months and months."

"No. This...whatever this is...it just started last night." Panic hit her again. This isn't how it was supposed to go. She could keep her emotions on an even level if he just went by the usual playbook. Why was he doing this?

He cocked his head to one side and studied her for a second. "What happened to the badass?"

"I have no idea what you mean."

His mouth twitched. "Damn, I would have never thought you would freak out just because I told you I loved you."

"I am not freaked out."

He leaned closer so that his breath feathered over her ear. "Liar."

It was a whisper that vibrated through her soul. He was right. She was lying.

When he pulled back, she wanted to protest, but instead, she pressed her lips together.

"Do you want to know when I started falling for you?"

She said nothing. She couldn't. His voice was deeper as if he remembered a moment...just one moment that changed his life.

"You came in one night. This was after you got shot protecting my sister-in-law. You were exhausted. You looked like you wanted to sleep for ten thousand years."

"So I looked like crap, and you fell in love? Sounds sus."

He took one hand in his. "You were exhausted, but you gave me crap about being from a firefighter family, but then you told me my Shepherd's pie was better than anyone else's—including your ma's."

"I complimented your food. Do you fall for every woman who says they like your food?"

"You don't remember what all you said."

She shook her head, but she was lying again.

"I won't call you a liar again, but I'll tell you. We were talking about that five-alarm fire at an apartment complex. You remember that one?"

She nodded. It had taken too many lives, including one firefighter.

"You asked if my brothers were there, and I said something like yeah, the heroes are at work. You stared me straight in the eye and told me that I did important work. My family agrees with you, by the way, but not everyone sees it that way. I get a lot of shit from some of the firefighters. You were different. You said, 'Just because you're not spraying your hose doesn't mean you aren't important, Declan. Giving people nourishment is vital, and you should be proud.'"

She blinked as the backs of her eyes started to burn. She would not cry.

"Maybe people think that way, but they don't say it. Even as you made an inappropriate joke about firefighters, you raised me up. I didn't realize it, but lust transformed into love. Right at that moment."

"Because I complimented you?"

"Not just me. I know you are the best tipper. They all tell me. I see the way you treat everyone. Like everyone belongs."

"Everyone has a role to play."

His mouth curled. "I fell in lust with you from the first moment I saw you. You stepped into my restaurant, all sassy and badassy, and those suits of yours." He rolled his eyes. "I must say, detective, you have the best ass I've ever seen. "

"Declan," she whispered, her face flaming. God, he made her blush by giving her a compliment.

"This is where you tell me how wonderful I am."

"It's fast."

He shook his head. "Doesn't matter. All that matters is that we're on the same page."

Fear rattled around in her chest as her heartbeat vibrated through her. She wasn't so much of a badass now, was she?

"Or, maybe you aren't."

"No. Wait. I am falling for you, Declan. It's just that I'm gun-shy on declarations. The last time I did it, I was in my twenties, and the guy couldn't handle me or my aspirations." It was her turn to study him. "You don't have a problem if I say I want to be the precinct captain?"

"What? Why would I? I'd be freaking proud of you. I have a feeling there haven't been many women who have done that."

She shook her head. "I'm one of the few women who even made it into homicide."

"See," he said as he brushed his mouth over hers, "definitely badass."

She settled a hand on his chest. His heart was beating as hard as hers was. "I come with the baggage of the job."

"Yeah. You also can't cook."

"Why did you come here tonight?"

"I had to see you."

"To tell me how to do my job? That I was wrong?"

He shook his head. "I would never tell you how to do your job. How could I? I'm just a chef."

"Shut up. You are not just a chef, Declan Matthew Fitzpatrick." She shook her head. "Jeez, you really are Irish, aren't you?"

"First, don't three name me. Second, you have no room to talk, Eileen. What did your parents do? Hear *Come On, Eileen*?" Heat stole over her cheeks, and he laughed. "No way!"

"Yes. It's embarrassing, considering what the song is about."

He set his forehead against hers. "But back to why I came here. I realized I truly cared about you beyond anything I've felt before. While I know you can handle yourself, I wanted to see you were okay with my own eyes."

She swallowed. "Thank you."

"For caring? It's as natural as breathing when it comes to you."

Her heart melted even more. The way it was going, it would land on the floor in a splat if he kept it up.

"No. For accepting me."

"Hey, not going to say I won't read you the riot act for putting a target on your back. Just know that I worry about you. I don't want to change you, but..." He drew in a deep breath. "It scared the hell out of me, that's all."

She opened her mouth, then snapped it shut. She knew that cost him a lot. From his staff to his charity work to his family, Declan took care of people. He wanted to care for her but was man enough to allow her to forge her way forward.

"I was planning on cooking dinner."

"You've cooked me food for the last twenty-four hours."

"I'd cook for you for a million years." He sighed. "Too soon, right?"

"We can eat. You can cook, or we can order. But after."

One eyebrow rose up. "After?"

She smiled. "Yeah, after."

He scooped her up out of the chair.

"Dude! You can't carry me up the stairs."

"I can, and I will."

Twelve

Need charged Declan's blood as he set Eileen on her feet beside her bed. Like the rest of her house, it felt like her, as if every corner breathed her essence.

With careful hands, he undressed Eileen. He knew he was a bastard for wanting to touch...to taste. She was exhausted, and he had kept her up the night before...but he needed this. His hands weren't steady, and he figured that was about right. She'd been knocking him off-kilter since they'd met.

It didn't take him long to get her naked. He stepped forward, cupping her face with one hand as he teased her nipple with the other. She pulled away from the kiss to lean her head back and moan. Damn, even in the dark room, he could see her, and it was one of the sexiest things he had ever seen.

Declan attacked her throat, kissing and nipping at her soft skin. For such a badass, she had skin like silk. She always smelled of roses, something else that wasn't what he'd expected. It wasn't something that overpowered his senses. It was just below the surface as if it were a part of her true self. The best part was knowing she was like this with him and not the world. She let everyone else see that steel spine of hers, but this…this was like a secret she only wanted a few people to see.

She gently pushed him away. Her hands went to the bottom of his shirt. Slowly, she eased it up his torso, her fingers sliding over his flesh. When it was lying on the floor with her clothes, she leaned forward to lick him down the center of his chest. Dropping to her knees, she undid his jeans and shoved them down. She made a sound of irritation.

"I keep thinking you'll be going commando, and you keep surprising me."

He chuckled. "Noted."

If she wanted him parading through the streets that surrounded the Inner Harbor on July 4th naked, he would do it. He was starting to realize there wasn't much he wouldn't do for this woman.

Soon, he was standing in front of her naked, his cock bobbing up against his abdomen. He was so fucking hard. He didn't think he would last even this long. Last night should have taken the edge off, but it didn't. It only made him want her more.

With sure, steady hands, she stroked his cock, then she took him into her mouth. At first, she teased the crown, wetting the head, then sliding her tongue around the edge before she sucked him into her mouth.

"Oh, damn, baby. That's good," he said as he speared his fingers through her hair.

Over and over, she sucked him into her mouth. His balls were heavy, and it was taking all he had not to come down her throat. With that thought, he tried to pull away, but she refused, sucking on him so hard his eyes rolled back in his head.

"Enough," he said, his voice dark even to his ears.

She kept him in her mouth and looked up at him. With one last lick, she let him go. He picked her up and practically threw her on the bed. She laughed, the sound filling the room. Later, he would revel in that sound, of the joy he gave her, but he was too close to the edge. He had to get inside of her as fast as possible.

He grabbed up his jeans to get a condom, then climbed on the bed with her. She had one hand on her breast and the other on her clit, watching him. This woman...she was so sensual, she made his teeth ache. He would never have lasted more than a week if he'd known what she was like.

Declan took her hips in his hands and flipped her over before he slipped a finger up her thigh to her sex. She was wet, dripping with need.

"Why, Detective O'Reilly, I think you liked sucking my cock."

Her inner muscles grabbed onto him. She liked the dirty talk, which was good because he planned on talking dirty to her a lot.

With somewhat unsteady hands, Declan ripped open the package, pulled out the condom, then rolled it on. He pulled her up and onto her knees. Taking her hips into his hands, he centered his dick at her entrance and thrust into her sex hard and fast.

Usually, he would take his time to enjoy the moment, but he didn't have his usual finesse. He wanted to mark her, to let her know that she was his and he was hers. He slammed into her, time and time again.

"Touch your clit, baby. I want to feel that pussy squeeze my dick."

She did as he ordered, moaning as she did. She was so

damned warm and snug. So when her muscles started to convulse around his shaft, he couldn't control himself any longer. His balls drew up, and that tell-tale tingle shot up his spine.

"Fuck, yes, Eileen." He shouted it so loudly there was a good chance the neighbors heard. He didn't care. He kept moving through his orgasm, and just as he was almost done, Eileen came again.

"Declan," she moaned.

A few moments later, Declan pulled out of her and then slipped into her bathroom so that he could throw out the condom. When he returned, she hadn't moved. In fact, he had to ease a half-awake Eileen up off her bed to get her under the sheets. He joined her. And just like the night before, she rolled into his arms.

As he drifted into a light sleep, he realized he wanted every night to be like this. Panic didn't rise up to choke him. Instead, a peace he hadn't ever felt before settled over him, and he drifted into a deeper sleep.

***

IT WASN'T until after midnight that they made it downstairs. They'd dozed after making love, but she'd wanted a shower, which turned into another crazy bout of sex. By the time they reached her kitchen, her stomach was growling. She'd thrown on a pair of sleep shorts and her BPD shirt that had seen better days. Before they headed downstairs, Declan pulled on his jeans and nothing else. He left his golden hair down, a mess from her hands. It made Eileen happy to know that. Like she had left a mark on him.

"I did notice you had eggs."

"I can boil an egg," she said indignantly.

"How about an omelet? You have some cheese in here."

"I do?"

He snorted. "We are gonna do something about your cooking skills."

"Please, don't go all 1950's Boomer on me. I'm never gonna be the little woman at home."

"Never said I wanted that. Grater?"

She pointed to the drawer behind him.

"I believe everyone should have basic cooking skills. Plus, I know that you're freaking amazing, and if you wanted to learn how to cook, you would. So, I will have to give you an incentive."

"And that would be?" Eileen asked as she caught sight of the box of goodies her neighbor had left her. She hoped it was her snickerdoodles because those were Eileen's favorite.

"Strip cooking."

"What?" She was momentarily distracted by the comment. "What is strip cooking?"

"I teach you, and every time you get a step right, I'll remove a piece of clothing."

She was laughing when she opened the package. She expected cookies or brownies. What she didn't expect was the polaroids of her victims. Icy fingers slipped down her spine as the ramifications crashed through her. He was at her house. Yes, she expected him to focus on her, but how had he gotten here before she got home?

"We could go the other way, and if you get things wrong..." His voice trailed off because he had turned to look at her. "Eileen?"

She shook her head, unable to speak. There weren't just two victims. There was a third. The polaroids were old, even stained, but she knew the woman.

With shaking hands, she grabbed her phone to call her partner.

"What? Don't you have a personal life?"

"Yeah, I was trying that, but our killer left a little package for me on my porch."

"What the hell?" Declan shouted as he walked around the island. She closed the box. He didn't need to see those. She wanted to protect him from this. From all the bad things in the world.

"I'll call it in and be there in a sec. Are you alone?"

"I know you just heard Declan. I'll check my security camera on the porch. I didn't get a notice that anyone showed up."

"Be there in fifteen."

He hung up before she could thank him.

She drew in a deep breath, trying to calm herself. The guy knew she was the detective on the case, so had he been thinking about contacting her?

"You need to get dressed."

That from Declan.

"Excuse me?"

"The cops will be here soon."

"I'm a cop."

His gaze slipped down her body. Oh, damn, he was right. "Let's get dressed. You won't be able to leave until you talk to Eddie. He'll want to question you."

Declan cocked his head and studied her. He was always

looking at her like he was trying to figure her out. "Why would I leave?"

Eileen opened her mouth, but he stepped closer and pulled her into his arms. "Is that what people do?"

"Messy situations are...you shouldn't be here."

He shouldn't. If she had a target on her back, he did too. What if the perp had zeroed in on her and wanted to hurt her by hurting Declan?

"I shouldn't? Why? Are you embarrassed to be seen with me?"

She snorted, then realized that he was serious. She lifted her arms and cupped his face.

"Declan, I am not embarrassed. It's just that this guy is targeting me. Anyone around me could get hurt."

There was a beat of silence. "You're worried about me?" She nodded. "Back at ya, O'Reilly."

"I can take care of myself."

"Never said you couldn't. Let's both get dressed so I don't have to punch anyone for staring at your legs."

She glanced at the box, then nodded.

"Why didn't you want me to look at them? I can handle things like that. You don't have to hide the ugly side of your work from me."

She looked at him, trying to come up with the right words. He didn't want to see them for the gore of it all. Declan wasn't someone who got into that.

"Irene is one of them. I didn't want you to see her that way. You cared about her. She was part of your family at Fitzpatrick's."

His gaze softened, and he nodded. A lump rose in her throat, and in that one instant, she knew she would do everything in her power to shield Declan from the horrors she saw every day.

She was also starting to realize she was definitely falling in love with the man. She wasn't quite sure what to do about that, but she knew he was right. Her coworkers would be there soon, and it would be best if they both got dressed.

"Let's go put on some clothes. I don't need techs drooling over that massive chest of yours."

"You're the only person I want to see my chest, Eileen."

She smiled as he followed her up the stairs. That was a good thing because she was starting to realize that she was feeling territorial about him, too. She'd have to figure out how to deal with it some other time. Right now, she had a nut job sending her weird photos.

Thirteen

By the time the cops got there, they were both dressed and ready for them. Her partner was first.

"Come on in," she said, stepping back. "My fingerprints will be on them. You made it here fast."

Eddie stopped, looked at her, then at Declan, and then back to Eileen.

"You're my partner, idiot."

Then he walked in. He took in the kitchen. Declan had put all the makings of an omelet away. Eileen had said she wasn't hungry. He would feed her later after this mess.

"Where did you find the box?"

"On my porch."

"When?"

"It was waiting for me when I got home."

Again, another look back and forth between them. Then, his gaze settled on Eileen. "Why didn't you call it right in?"

"I didn't open it."

"What? You got a package on your porch with no markings

and no return address, and you just set it down and forgot about it?"

Anger vibrated from Eddie's voice, and while Declan knew her partner was worried about her, he did not like how he talked to her.

"I think you need to watch your tone."

Eileen and Eddie both looked at him. Eddie looked amused, and Eileen looked irritated. Damn, she was pretty when she was irritated.

"Sure thing, Fitzpatrick." There was a knock at the door. "Why don't you go let the techs in? I only called in a few people."

She nodded.

"Why?"

"The less people who know about this, the better. We don't want any wannabes coming out of the woodwork targeting Eileen."

The knocking had stopped, then started again. He turned to get them, but he stopped by Eileen and brushed his mouth over hers. Then, he went to the door. A man and woman stood there.

"We're here for the crime scene."

"Badges?"

The man frowned and opened his mouth to complain. The woman pulled out her badge. It read Jillian Roberts.

"That's me, and I vouch for Walters. Francisco said there was something we had to take care of here."

"Come on in," he said, stepping back and giving them room. "They're in the kitchen at the end of the hall."

Jillian nodded, and the two of them stopped to put booties on.

"Just an FYI, it's only a box with pictures."

The two shared a look, then abandoned putting on the booties. They walked down the hall, and he followed.

"Eileen?" Jillian asked.

"Hey, Jill, Ned. The only person who touched the box was me. My fingerprints will be on the pictures." She looked at Declan, then made her way over to him. "You can leave after you talk to Eddie."

He shook his head. "Nope." Once again, he brushed his mouth over hers. "I'll answer his questions, then wait."

He turned and walked into the living room without letting her dismiss him again.

When Eddie finally caught up with him, her partner was smiling at him. "Perfect way to play it, man."

"Not playing at anything." He couldn't keep the anger out of his voice.

Eddie's eyes widened. "I didn't mean in a bad way. I think most men let her boss them around. You refusing to leave is a good thing. That's all. No need to get pissed."

"So, I'm not supposed to get pissed at the fact that Eileen is being targeted by some maniac? Because you and I both know that's what those pictures are."

"Did you see them?"

"No. I saw the box. She thought it was goodies from the crazy lady next door."

Francisco nodded, telling Declan that he was confirming the story. Which pissed him off. "She's not lying to you."

"I didn't say she was, but we have to confirm the story. That way, everything is above board. My worry is that the box got here before she got home."

"Well, since she challenged him on TV, it isn't that insane that he decided to do this."

There was a beat of silence. "This was planned."

"Well, yes."

"Before the asshole saw her on TV. Add that someone disabled her doorbell camera. That seems thought out. As in, no matter what, that box was getting here tonight. He wanted that contact."

Declan swallowed, and his blood turned frigid. He didn't know much about police work, but from what he had seen in TV shows and movies, it was never good when the bad guy was super focused on one person.

"Yeah. I see that you understand the situation. She's gonna try and push you away."

"Fuck that."

Eddie chuckled. "Good. Eileen is the best partner I've ever had. She's smart and always works hard. She needs people in her corner."

Declan nodded because he planned on being in that corner for as long as she would have him. He was starting to realize that, for him, this was it. He was ready to pledge his entire life to her, but he knew better than to tell her that. Eileen had too much on her plate at the moment.

"You said you didn't see the pics?"

"No. She set the box on the counter. We were busy. Then we came back downstairs to eat."

"She had food in her fridge?"

Declan found his first little smile since Eileen called her partner.

"Eggs and cheese."

"But you never saw the pics."

"She wouldn't let me see them."

Eddie nodded. "Yeah, that makes sense."

"Would you let your wife see them?"

"Yeah, but she's a prosecutor. She's seen a lot of gore. If it had been someone she knew, probably not. Or I would try. But, as I said, she's not exactly a civilian."

"She prosecutes murderers?"

"Sometimes, but she mainly handles sex crimes."

"Damn."

"And she's not happy about this. She wants to call out the entire apparatus from Baltimore PD up through the federal law enforcement, but we want to keep it on the down low."

"Why?"

"Because the bastard wants the attention. Eileen's not going to give it to him. She agrees with me, by the way. It's bad enough the press has given him a name."

"What the hell? Why didn't you tell me?" Eileen said from the doorway.

"Sorry. I was so irritated with the situation I forgot."

"What are they calling him?" Declan asked.

"The Fleet Street Slasher. People are already making the link."

The partners shared a look. Something cold and heavy settled in Declan's stomach.

"What link?"

"There was a murder in 1987."

He frowned. "They're linked?"

"Eddie, he doesn't need to know about this."

"He does if he's going to hang with you, and since he was with you during the two recent murders, we know that he has a perfect alibi."

"Fine. A young woman named Norma Wilson was murdered just off Fleet Street. Stabbed. An ornate handle on the knife. No killer was ever found."

"Eileen has been looking into it for years."

There was a knock at the door, and Eddie turned to answer it.

"Sure, just go right ahead and answer my door."

He flipped her off as he opened the door. There were noises of more cops. Eddie was giving them information on where to search, and Eileen frowned. There was something about her reaction that bothered him.

"What?"

She shook her head and stepped closer to him. Soon, the door was shut, and Eddie was walking back in.

"What is Bryan doing here?"

"He was hanging with his cousin Allen when he got the call."

"Who is Bryan?"

Eddie smiled. "One of Eileen's many exes."

"I don't have that many exes, and we dated a decade ago when we were both at the academy."

"She kicked his ass there and made detective before him."

He filed that bit of information away.

"Are we done arguing that there is a connection?" Eddie asked.

"No. We are not."

"Eileen, there is a pic of Norma. One that wasn't in evidence."

"Who even has Polaroids anymore?" she muttered as if lost in thought.

"Maybe the killer is one and the same. Maybe the same camera," Eddie commented.

"This guy isn't the doer for that one. Even if he had been just eighteen then, he would be in his mid-fifties."

"He would physically be able to do it."

"Yes, but think about it. Irene was a smart woman. She wouldn't walk down the street with an older man like that. And from what the other people told us, she was dating someone."

"Yeah, I heard a few of my crew talking about it," Declan said.

"But no one saw him," she said.

He nodded.

"This was a good guy. A guy with a job, not one staring down retirement. She had no daddy complex. This is not the same guy. Also, the women are different. Killers can change their MO, but that much?" She shook her head. "I don't think so."

"That's worse."

Her partner's comment had him blinking.

When Eileen looked away from Francisco, Declan knew she agreed. "What am I missing?"

"Eileen?" Eddie asked, waving his hand.

He was going to let Eileen tell Declan.

"Eddie thinks that if he is obsessed with that crime, it might have something to do with me. Which is a possibility, but it could be that I'm the one on the case."

Panic swamped him. He knew her job was dangerous, but having a serial killer obsessed with her? No. That was not acceptable.

"Most people have forgotten about that crime, Eileen."

"No, they haven't. My mother's class just did a bunch of social media about it. They do it every damned year."

"Your mother's class?" Declan asked.

She nodded. "She was my mother's English teacher. She's actually the reason my mother is a teacher."

Eddie was frowning at her. "I think you need to go to a safe house."

She rolled her eyes. "I don't need to do that. He could have done it before Declan showed up if he wanted to get me. He didn't."

"I could go above your head."

"It's a good way to lose yours."

Oh, damn, Eileen just threatened her partner. He didn't look scared. More annoyed.

"Listen, once everything is done here, why don't we go to my place?" Declan suggested. His nerves were already raw. Worry might cloud his judgment, but he knew it was a good idea. "I'm relatively new in your life, and he might not know much about me. A lot of people don't know where I live."

"Why is that?" Eddie asked, who was now eyeing him suspiciously.

He held up his hands. "I have a PO Box. Officially, my apartment is my address, but that's the restaurant's address. It confuses a lot of people."

"He's right," Eddie said with a nod. "Plus, you don't have shit to eat in this house, as usual."

She made a rude sound. "I'd like to know what your bachelor fridge looked like."

"Leftovers from my mom."

She rolled her eyes.

"Eddie," Jillian called out.

"Excuse me."

He left them alone. The air was heavy as if a lot needed to be said, but he didn't know how long they had before Francisco returned.

"I can stay at my parents' or maybe Zac's."

"Not Zane?"

"Ugh, no. He only has things like protein bars to eat."

"Your family has food issues."

She laughed, but her smile soon faded. "I'm sorry."

"For what? For having a psycho target you? What would you say to any other victim?"

"I am not a victim."

He disagreed, but he let that go. "Either way doesn't matter. You are staying with me until you find out who the hell this guy is and lock him away."

"I can't let you do that."

"Well, you will. I need to do this." He stepped closer, taking her by the hips. It had been less than an hour since they'd made love before this bastard had tried to ruin everything. "Let me do this one thing for you."

She nodded. "If you can tell me why."

"Why I'm doing this?"

"Yes."

"Easy. I love you."

"No, you don't. You said you were falling in love."

"I did not." He shook his head as he smiled at her. Again, her terror at having him love her shouldn't amuse him, but it did. Maybe it was the knowledge that she seemed to be as knocked off kilter as much as he was by her. "I said I love you, but we'll go with it. I'm falling in love with you if it makes you feel better."

"Fine."

"Pack enough for a couple of days. That way, you don't have to come back here unless you want to."

She nodded, then looked up at him. "You're not always going to get your way."

"As long as I have you, that's all that matters."

Her eyes softened, and she leaned up on her tiptoes to kiss him. "Thanks."

"I'll always be in your corner."

Someone called for her. She sighed. When she looked up at him again, regret filled her gaze. She moved away from him, and he let her go. She knew he had her back, and that was all that mattered at that moment.

Fourteen

Over an hour later, Eileen stomped into Declan's apartment. "This is stupid."

The man said nothing. Instead, he hummed as he headed over to his kitchen.

"Declan!"

"Yes, my love?"

"Don't you 'my love' me."

"I like calling you that."

She wanted to scream. The man was driving her batty. Worse, the captain had gotten wind of the situation and told her she was not to come in tomorrow. Or today, seeing how it was past midnight.

"This is stupid. I shouldn't stay with you. I should stay far away from you."

He pulled out what looked like the makings of an omelet. "You're right."

Her heart sank a little. He agreed with her. "Oh."

"Don't look like that, love. Do you want any kind of meat or veggies in your omelet?"

"If you are making an omelet, why didn't we stay at my house?"

Again, he was watching her in that way of his. It was like he had her all figured out. How did the man look so good? She was sure she was a mess, her hair was probably all over the place, and he was standing there with perfect hair.

He stepped around the counter and pulled her into his arms.

"Which thing do you want me to address first? The staying with me or the omelet thing?" She didn't respond. "First, you had eggs and cheese, but I have more choice of ingredients. Otherwise, you would end up at a safe house or with a guard."

"A guard?"

He nodded. "I heard that Bryan guy offer to guard you."

"No thanks."

"Yeah, that asshole wasn't getting near you."

Then he kissed her nose and went to work in the kitchen.

"I want you to take this seriously, Declan."

"I am. I would like to find the bastard and string him up, but I'm not trained for that. So instead, I'll cook your food and give you a place to stay because you are the badass in this situation who will catch him."

Her phone went off with Eddie's ringtone.

She grabbed it up. "What do you want?"

"I was thinking."

"And?"

"We need to look into the legacies."

"Why?"

"Think about it. People could find out who was running the investigation, but only someone in the station house or at least in law enforcement would know how to find you so fast."

"Not in today's online world."

"You have no social media. You keep offline. It would take a lot of digging to find you so fast and make that connection. Have you given any interviews about the first murder?"

"Irene's?"

"No, Norma's."

"No. I stayed out of it on purpose."

"So people knew you were checking out the files and looking into it."

She sighed. "Damn, don't know why I didn't think about that. There are so many."

"Yeah. I'll get the info discreetly and come to your boyfriend's house tomorrow."

"Okay. Text me when you're close. Oh, and did Bryan offer to act as my guard?"

"Yeah. That dude has issues. He thought he would show up at your house and be all manly. Seeing Declan there probably put a crimp in his plans."

"Thanks, Eddie."

She hung up.

"So, Eddie had news."

"Not really. Just a passing thought that only a few people would be able to find out that I was looking into the old homicide. I didn't post anywhere about it—I don't have social media."

"Yeah, I know."

"And how would you know that, Mr. Fitzpatrick?"

He chuckled. "I might have looked around."

Since she had watched his short cooking videos a time or two, she couldn't say anything to that. "Anyway, we thought it might have to be someone from law enforcement. I wasn't officially assigned the case, but I looked into it and checked out the files."

"Ah."

"And that means it could be a legacy, or it could just be someone in the precinct." She shrugged. She hated to think it could be another cop, but it kind of made sense. The guy had avoided all CCTV, and he seemed to know the intimate details of Irene's murder.

"So, why don't you turn it off just for a few minutes while you eat this," he said, setting a plate on the counter in front of her. It was probably the most perfect omelet she had ever seen in her life. How did he do that?

"You want anything to drink with it?"

She looked up at him. "Yeah...just some water would be great."

"You sit right there and let me take care of you. Then we can get to bed, and you can get some rest."

She wanted to argue, but her stomach protested.

"Eddie will be here before you know it, and you can start obsessing again."

He was right. She would think more clearly if she had some rest. So, she decided to give in to the amazing food he'd cooked for her and then get that rest.

EDDIE WALKED INTO THE PRECINCT. He'd been home, unable to sleep, because something was nagging at him. Marguerite had ordered him back to work because he was disturbing her beauty sleep. Something was always happening at a police station, especially in a city like Baltimore. They had their share of crime, so it was hard to get any privacy there. Still, at least there is less activity at night.

As he sat at his desk, he pulled open his laptop. There was something that was bothering him about this case. It just wouldn't leave him alone. The fact that someone had tied that old cold case in was weird. It was like this case wasn't about these women...or not only about them. They had been picked because they resembled the first victim, but they also looked like...fuck.

Yeah, he should have picked up on this. The perp was fixated on Eileen. This killing spree might have been inspired by her. But why? He knew that she hadn't dated anyone in the last few months, and from what she'd said, she had been pretty focused on her rehab from being shot and then getting back to work. Now, though...there was something off.

"Francisco, what are you doing here?"

He looked up to find the captain walking into the bullpen.

"Couldn't sleep. I'm connecting things on this case, and I don't like it."

He nodded with his head towards his office. "Let's talk about it because I am too. Before we talk to her, I want to get on the same page."

Mathers didn't have to say who the *her* was. Eddie did as the captain suggested and followed him into his office.

"Someone who knows her," he said as he shut the door.

It wasn't a question. It was a statement from his captain.

"Someone *here* who knows her. It wasn't known outside the precinct that she was working on that cold case."

The captain sighed and settled in his chair behind his desk. "So you don't think it's the same person?"

Eddie shook his head. "Eileen doesn't either. Or, at least, she didn't. She was basing it on the fact that Irene might have dated the perp."

Another long sigh. "That means we need someone here who might have been dating the victim and had a connection to Eileen."

He nodded as something nudged at his brain. Something that he couldn't seem to grasp.

"You thought of something."

He rubbed a hand over his face, trying to concentrate. "I'm exhausted, and my brain is trying to shut down. I know that we would do better with Eileen here."

"I heard Comstock wanted to be her guard," Mathers said with a chuckle. "That boy done fucked up years ago with her, and he has never accepted it."

Eddie straightened. "Fuck. Comstock."

He shot up out of his chair and hurried out to his desk.

Mathers followed him out. "What?"

"Comstock. He's been all up in her business. Eileen admitted to me that she told him way back at the academy that she wanted to solve the case for her mother."

"That's a long time for him to be planning this."

"Yeah. Now he has one uncle, right? The one that helped him get to detective?"

He sensed Mathers' nod. "But there was another one, wasn't there? He died a few months ago?"

"Yeah, it was the reason Bryan got detective, in a way. Spot came open and his other uncle pushed for him to move ahead."

Eddie started to click through the files. Eileen shared some of the files with him, wanting his opinion. He pulled up the acquaintances of Norma. The moment he saw the name, ice coated his bones. "Fuck. We need to get people out to Fitz-patrick's."

He was calling Eileen when he heard the captain ordering units to the address. He just hoped that bastard wasn't there yet.

EILEEN WOKE AROUND FOUR, not sure what woke her up. Maybe she had started getting conditioned to early mornings. She and Eddie seemed to get calls a lot around that time of the morning. She turned her head and looked at Declan. He was sleeping, a big, sexy bear of a man, and he loved her. He looked so peaceful, his face relaxed. Trying not to disturb him, she slipped out of bed and headed for the kitchen. She needed a drink of water.

She slipped on one of his t-shirts, then tiptoed to the kitchen. After grabbing a glass, she turned toward the refriger-ator and opened it. Then, she sensed someone in the room with her—and she knew it wasn't Declan. Don't ask her how she did, but she knew.

"Don't," he said.

Eileen looked over in the direction of the voice. Bryan stood there, all dressed in black. It took her a moment or two to comprehend what she was seeing.

"What the fuck are you doing here?"

"I've come to save you."

She frowned, thinking about what they had said about him wanting to guard her. "I don't need help, but thanks."

"You have no idea how dangerous he is to you."

"He?"

"*Fitzpatrick.*" He spat out the word like it was poison.

"What the hell are you talking about?"

"You weren't meant for him. We were meant to be together."

"Again, what the hell are you talking about? We dated for a couple of months years ago. We were not right for each other."

"We were perfect." He stepped closer, and that's when she saw the gun and the zip ties.

"No. Remember? You hated the idea that I did better than everyone."

His face flushed with anger. "Yes, but that was before I knew about our connection."

"You're losing me again."

"My uncle was who you were looking for. All those years, you've been searching for the man who killed Norma, and it was my Uncle Simon."

In that instant, she remembered a rumor that Norma had known a cop, but there was nothing to substantiate the rumor. Simon Culpepper was Bryan's uncle on his mother's side of the family and had worked their precinct.

"So," he gave her a smile. Eileen was sure he thought it was teasing, but every creep alarm went off in her head. "I gave you similar women. They were prettier than the ones Uncle Simon killed. And now you know we should be together."

The nut job thought she would love the fact he was killing women who looked like her. Still, she had to reason with him. If she convinced Bryan that she would go with him before Declan woke up, she could protect him. She could not take a chance that he would walk out here. That might send Bryan over the edge.

"Yes," she said, nodding and smiling at him. "Definitely we should be together."

His smile widened. The demented look in his eyes sent prickles racing along her skin. He was insane. Truly. He actually thought she would be happy with all of this.

"I'll need to get dressed."

He nodded. "And I need to kill Fitzpatrick."

"No," she said, trying to keep her fear at bay. She needed to make sure that Bryan stayed far away from Declan. Her ex was on the edge of insanity and might pop off at any time. "Why do you want to mess with him? He doesn't matter. You're all that matters."

"But if he's alive, our love will be tainted."

She had moved so that she was facing Declan's room and Bryan's back was to it.

"No. Our love could never be tainted. It's too pure."

She almost threw up after saying that, but she fought it. She had to keep this idiot engaged until she could get him out of there and away from Declan.

For a moment, Bryan's eyes softened as he stared at her with that creepy smile...then there was a creak behind him as if someone were walking around Declan's bedroom.

Shit. She knew that she couldn't distract Bryan anymore. Declan was moving around, and if Bryan thought he was awake, he would see him as a threat. Bryan turned toward the sound, his eyes going cold in that instant, and she knew this was her only chance.

Eileen rushed him, launching her entire body at Bryan, hoping her forward motion would catch him by surprise. She apparently did because he had no chance to prepare himself to get hit by her, and they both went tumbling down.

"What the fuck!" Bryan growled as he hit the floor face-first.

She heard the clatter of his gun and knew that he'd lost control of it.

He reared up, sending her tumbling to the floor. She hit her head so hard on the wooden floor that stars formed before her eyes. Hell, she was even hearing sirens.

"You fucking bitch!" Bryan screamed as he wrapped his hands around her neck.

She struggled against him, clawing at his hands but he was so strong, and she was losing the ability to fight him. The roar she heard made her ears ring, and in the next instant, Bryan's fingers jerked away, and his body weight was gone.

She was able to draw in a deep breath, then two. The sounds of flesh hitting flesh filled the room as she heard the door downstairs bust open.

"You. Don't. Touch. Her." It was Declan punching Bryan. He was straddled on top of her ex, hitting him with each word he said.

It took her a second or two before she could stand and approach him. Bryan was close to being unconscious. His nose was broken, his lip bloody.

"Declan, babe," she grabbed his arm as she heard footsteps coming up the stairs. "Don't kill him."

Declan turned to her. Anger and just more than a bit of violence filled his gaze. Eileen could tell he didn't want to let go of Bryan, but soon Eddie was in the room with tons of uniforms, and Jesus, Mathers was there too.

"They can handle him."

He blinked and looked over at Eddie, who was staring at Declan with admiration. Then, he released Bryan and rose. The next instant, he pulled her into his arms. She was so close to crying, which was so out of the normal for her she fought it. She would not cry in front of her boss and partner.

She could hear them reading Bryan his rights, so she assumed he was finally conscious.

"Damn, he's gonna need paramedics," Eddie said. He looked over at them. "I kept calling, but you didn't pick up."

"Eileen needs—f"

Declan didn't get to finish his comment.

"Of course I want up there, asshole," someone downstairs yelled. "That's my brother's place, and I want to make sure everything is okay."

"Emmet's here," he said. "I'll have him look at you. Why don't you go in and get dressed?"

"I can't."

"What?"

"They'll need evidence."

More loud stomping feet. Her head was pounding, and her throat hurt, and she felt slightly nauseous. Damn. That could mean she had a concussion, and if she did, they would probably make her go to the hospital.

"Don't worry. Emmett will check you out, but you and I both know that you're probably headed to the hospital."

She looked up at him. "I don't want to go."

"Too bad." Then, he kissed her nose.

"I can't believe you threw a party and didn't invite me, brother," Emmet said. She looked over at him and saw nothing but concern in his eyes.

"I don't want to go to the hospital."

"You will go if Emmet says you have to. But I'll be with you."

She didn't like it, but if Declan would be there, she decided she could deal with it. She figured she could deal with just about anything with him beside her. She just hoped that this insanity didn't chase him off.

Fifteen

By the time Declan made it up to Eileen's room, it felt like hours had passed. He'd ridden with her to the hospital, but she had insisted he get his knuckles looked at. They'd been bloody from hitting Comstock, and it had been worth it. While she had to have an MRI and be examined by the doctor, along with having evidentiary pictures taken of her injuries, he hurried to get his stuff done.

On his way up the first time, Eddie had stopped him because Declan had to make a statement about the attack. Now, he was more than a little irritated because he had told Eileen he would be with her. When he reached her floor, he found the twins outside her room talking to Wendy. When they showed up, Wendy had been on staff in the trauma center.

"Hey," Wendy said, hugging him. "So glad you're safe."

He returned her hug, then stepped back. The twins were dressed in jeans and long-sleeved t-shirts. They both looked worried and pale.

"We heard you kicked his ass," Zane said. His hair was

shorter than Zac's, which was the only way he could tell them apart.

He shrugged. "I punched him a few times."

"I always hated that guy," Zac said.

"Yeah. Always thought he was a douche. Definitely something off there. I should have realized it."

The door opened, and an older man frowned out at them. "Boys, you're making too much noise."

They weren't, but he saw the worry weighing on the man's shoulders. The moment he made eye contact with Declan. Without a doubt, this was Eileen's father. Just under six feet, he had a ton of salt and pepper hair, and he had her eyes.

"Is this him?" he asked his sons.

"Yeah," Zane said.

He held out his hand. "I'm Declan Fitzoomph—"

Mr. O'Reilly was hugging him so hard he thought he might lose consciousness. "Thank you for saving my girl. She's tough, but I'm glad she had you there."

"John, you're smothering him," someone said. When her dad finally released Declan, he could see the woman who had spoken. Small in stature, she wore her hair short no-nonsense, just like her daughter, and she smiled at Declan. Oh, damn. That was Eileen's smile.

"Declan, Eileen has been worried about you. She didn't understand what was taking you so long. I also believe she sent her partner a rather bad text that involved profanity. She's agitated and won't be happy until you get in there."

He nodded. "Thanks."

"No. Thank you for being there for her. Just a warning, she is quite cranky about having to stay overnight. She even tried to get Wendy to help her escape."

He looked at his sister-in-law. "I reminded her that she wouldn't help me when I had a concussion."

"Thanks, sis," he said. She had been like a sister to all of them, with the exception of Aeden, for years. Before he could finally get in the room, there was a bit of commotion down the hall near the nurse's station. He turned and found his family. From the look of the grouping, the only people missing were Kaitlin and little Mike.

"There he is," Emmet said, not using his indoor voice. Declan cringed.

"I hope you still think good things about me after you meet my family," he murmured to Eileen's mother.

They moved en masse down the hall, the buzz of their voices filling the once-quiet space. The moment she stepped in front of him, his mother grabbed him.

"Tell me you kicked that man's ass."

Yep, his mother could be bloodthirsty when one of her family had been threatened.

"He did," Zac said as he stepped up beside him. "I heard from some of the cops that Eileen had to pull him off the bastard."

Her gaze moved from Declan to Eileen's brother. "You're one of the twins."

"Zac, and this is my brother Zane. And, of course, our parents, John and Rhonda O'Reilly."

Introductions were made, but as everyone was talking, Rhonda took him aside. "Go on. My girl will feel better if she gets to see you."

"Thanks," he said, not needing to be told twice. He slipped into her room. She had a private room. All the lights were set to dim, and she appeared to be dozing, which he knew went against the concussion protocol.

He stepped closer and studied her, his anger rolling over him again. He knew she could handle herself, but the fact that she now had bruises on her neck made him want to punch Bryan Comstock again.

"Stop gritting your teeth," she said without opening her eyes.

"You're awake," he said, then rolled his eyes. She had just spoken, so of course, she was awake.

"Kind of hard not to be awake with all that commotion. What's going on?"

"My family showed up."

Her mouth curved, and her eyelids flickered before opening. "They are rowdy, but then so are the O'Reillys."

He walked forward, then sat on the bed beside her.

"Thank you." Her voice was still hoarse.

"For what?"

"You saved me."

"If you had been in a safe house, he might not have gotten to you."

She shook her head. "One way or another, it would come to a head. I'm just glad you were there."

He took her hand in his. Tonight, she looked even more delicate. "Me too."

"They don't want me sleeping long."

"How long?"

"They want me to wake up every half hour, which I find excessive."

He couldn't stop the chuckle that bubbled up. This woman, she was it for him. She'd almost been choked to death and had a concussion, and she was fussing.

"Tell you what, love." Her eyes softened. "You sleep, and I'll ensure you wake up like they want you to."

"Thank you," she whispered. "I was afraid."

"He wouldn't have been able to kill you."

"No. I was worried he would hurt you. He kept talking about killing you. I can't lose you, Declan. I refuse."

"I like that attitude." He leaned forward and brushed his mouth over her forehead. "Now sleep."

She sighed and settled further into her bed. Within moments, her breathing evened out. Declan pulled out his phone and set the timer for thirty minutes, then he sat in the chair beside her bed, her hand in his.

———

TWO DAYS LATER, Eileen was finally home. The doctors had been worried about the concussion, which was worse than they'd first thought. It sucked that she was stuck at the hospital and not interviewing Bryan. But thankfully, she was allowed to sleep for however long she wanted to.

When she and Declan walked into the kitchen, she stopped. The entire island was covered with cookies, muffins, and breads.

"That's nothing. You should see what you have in the fridge."

She glanced at him, her heart turning over in her chest. The fact that he had stood by her, taken care of her, and run interference when friends and family got to be too much had meant more to her than anything else. She wasn't usually so antisocial, but all the noise still hurt her head.

When she opened the fridge, she found it stocked with all kinds of food.

"Your family, mine, my kitchen, and the Santinis all brought food. We'll need to put some in the freezer, or they will go to waste."

She nodded and shut the door.

"Want to tell me about it? Can you?"

Eddie had stopped by the hospital before she was discharged. Bryan had come prepared that night. He'd come with weapons and a cell jammer.

"Simon was always a problem. I never met him, but I heard he never made it up the chain because there was always something off about him. Never married. He was engaged once, but she broke it off. Simon liked to slap her around when he was drunk."

She sighed.

"We don't have to go over this."

"No. I'm just trying to wrap my head around it. Six months ago, Simon died, and Bryan got the bulk of his uncle's belongings, which included a storage locker."

She swallowed, thinking about the pictures Eddie had shown her. "Simon was evil, and, apparently, when Bryan found all the proof that his uncle was a killer, he decided to go that route. It's hard to believe, but now that I think back, there had to be a reason I never slept with him."

"That killer lurking beneath the surface?"

Eileen nodded. "I know that when Bryan found out about his uncle, it was a trigger moment, but that instinct had to be there beneath the surface."

She wondered if he would even end up in prison. He was on suicide watch at the moment. That was her past. She looked up at Declan. This man, he was her future. He was her everything.

"What?"

"I was just thinking that we haven't discussed what would happen after all this."

"Do you have to? I mean, do we have to decide?"

She shook her head, a smile curving her lips. "As long as you want to stick around."

He snorted. "Try to get rid of me, O'Reilly."

This man. He let her be tough, but he also let her show her soft side. He accepted her just as she was. Taking his hand, she led him out of the kitchen.

"Where are we going?"

She tossed a smile over her shoulder. His eyes turned darker, his need easy for her to see. It was the same desire sparking through her blood. She needed this, needed him.

He let out a whoop and picked her up bridal style. "Don't ever let it be said that I didn't do everything in my power to please you."

She wrapped her arms around his neck. "I love you."

"I love you," he said, then he carried her up the stairs and into the rest of their lives.

THE FITZPATRICKS

Epilogue

"I can't believe you made me burn my muffins," Eileen groused at him.

Declan tried not to laugh, but she looked so cute. They were in their kitchen—yep, he had moved in that day after she came from the hospital and never left—and he was trying his best to teach her how to bake banana nut muffins. It was not going well.

It had been six months since that horrible night, but it was just a whisper—like a bad dream they had shared. Bryan pleaded out so Eileen didn't have to be part of a trial. She was disappointed because she wanted to face off against him in court, but Declan didn't want her near the man.

"How is it *my* fault?" he asked.

She turned to him and let one eyebrow rise up as she crossed her arms beneath her breasts. God, she was pretty. He loved it when she looked at him in that badass way. And yes, she had just been screaming his name. Declan had had her up on the island, his head between her legs, and they had both missed the timer going off.

"Okay, but you know...I was doing it to please you."

She rolled her eyes, but he knew she wasn't really mad. In fact, it had been her fault they were in this situation. His plan to do strip baking had never worked. One way or another, she would convince him to get completely naked before they accomplished anything. It wasn't that hard to achieve that because he was always ready to get naked with her.

"We can try it again."

She shook her head. "Nope. I'm done baking."

This had been something they went through all the time.

"Not fair. I had to learn how to shoot a gun."

He did not like that, but it was part of her job, so he tried it.

"Fine, but maybe I could get better at something else."

He picked her up by her waist and set her on the kitchen island again. Maybe this time, he would follow through with his plans.

"What am I supposed to tell our children?"

Her mouth twitched. "Are you pregnant, Declan?"

"No, but I don't want to say I couldn't teach my wife how to bake."

She opened her mouth to blast him, but he pulled out the ring he bought five months earlier. Declan had wanted to propose to her for months, but he had never felt the time was right. Now that everything was done with the case that brought them together, he felt okay with proposing. And he was ready to start the next chapter of their life together.

"Will you marry me, Eileen?"

He opened the box to reveal a square diamond. Simply elegant, just like the love of his life. The longer she stared at it and said nothing, his confidence frayed.

"Eileen?"

When she looked up at him, tears filled her eyes.

"Okay, no. I take it back."

She blinked. "What?"

"I'm sorry I made you cry. Pretend I didn't propose to you."

He tried to snap the ring box close, but she grabbed it.

"There is no takesy backsies."

Tears streamed down her cheeks, and he wanted it to stop. It was breaking his damned heart.

"I can if it makes you that miserable."

She shook her head. "I'm not miserable."

"Then, why are you crying?"

She swallowed as she held the ring box against her chest as if it were the most precious thing in the world. "I'm happy. I was hoping our relationship was leading to this, but I wasn't sure."

He leaned forward and set his forehead against hers. "This was always the plan. I just wanted to make sure I didn't spook you."

She sighed, but it was filled with happiness. "Good." She pulled back and opened the box. "It's pretty."

"Just like my woman."

Her mouth curved. He never got sick of that. A simple gesture could bring her so much joy. Declan had discovered that Eileen was more like him than he thought when they first met. Their happiness was found in the simple things, and they didn't need big gestures to prove their love to each other.

"So, is that a yes or a no?"

She looked up at him, her eyes filled with those happy tears. "Yes. Always. I love you, Declan, even if you are a crappy shot."

Declan chuckled as he took the box from her hands and slipped the ring on her finger. "And I love you, even if you burn everything you put your hands on."

He cupped her face and kissed her, with the smell of burnt muffins surrounding them and the warmth of their love filling their home. Always.

———

THANK you so much for reading Declan and Eileen's story! If you loved it, please think about leaving a rating or review at your favorite online store or review site. Reviews and ratings help other readers find my books and I truly appreciate it.

The first book in the Fitzpatricks Series is At Last, and features Wendy and Aeden. Make sure to check out the first chapter.

The Fitzpatrick family made their first appearance in One Night with a Santini, Santinis Book 8. Read the first chapter here.

At Last

She never thought she would find love.

Wendy knows that having money doesn't always make for a happy childhood. Hers was filled with nannies and disapproval from most of her family. That's why she lets guys know from their first date that there won't be a future. If her own flesh and blood thinks she's unlovable, how would a man be able to love her? What she wasn't prepared for was Aeden Fitzpatrick, who blows away all her plans to stay single in one long, amazing night.

Their chemistry is off the charts and for the first time, she finds it hard to leave a man, but she has obligations.

She's a woman who has always gotten under his skin.

Aeden knows he shouldn't want Wendy. She's his baby sister's best friend and annoyed him for the longest time. Snooty and a know-it-all, she knew just how to irritate him. Of course, it didn't mean that he wouldn't fantasize about her. And sure, there was the irrational hatred for every man she had ever dated.

But then...the night of his sister's wedding changes everything. Now, all he wants to do is keep her close, but she's on her way overseas.

A twisted obsession could tear them apart.

Six months later, her return not only gains his attention, but she's now a local celebrity. Unfortunately, she's also acquired a stalker, someone who wants to hurt her. As the threats turn sinister, Aeden becomes determined to do anything in his power to keep her safe–even sacrifice himself.

Wendy stared at herself in the mirror above the bathroom sink at Fitzpatrick's Bar and Grill. There were no more signs of the crying jag she'd been through. She knew going to Africa to work for six months was going to be hard, but it was something she wanted to do. And, she needed to do it. For herself.

It probably wasn't the best idea to tell her pregnant friend at said friend's reception that she was leaving Tuesday. Lord, what had she been thinking? It was a mistake of the first order, but she hadn't had much time to prepare. One person had to return to the US, and she could fill the slot. She had no significant other, and her blood relatives wouldn't even know. The Fitzpatricks, her best friend's family and now her adoptive family, would understand. Fitzpatricks served.

She took one last look in the mirror to reassure herself that she no longer looked horrible then she picked up her purse and headed out. She opened the door and ran directly into a large, warm, figure.

Without looking up, she knew it was Aeden Fitzpatrick. It drove her crazy that he had this much effect on her.

"Whoa," he said, grabbing her by the forearms. She looked up, and his smile turned to a frown.

"Why have you been crying?"

"Dammit. I thought I cleaned up the mess."

"You didn't answer the question. Did one of the Santinis make a move on you?"

She wanted to laugh. Kaitlin, her best friend, and Aeden's sister had just married Brando Santini. He came with a whole group of sexy brothers and cousins. All of them had flirted, but none of them had been disrespectful. From what she gathered, there would be hell to pay from one of the Santini mamas if they didn't behave.

"No."

"I saw you dancing with that cowboy."

"Yeah. I also danced with all your brothers. I don't see you having a problem with that."

"They think of you as a sister."

The heavy moment before seemed to evaporate. "Ah, so you all find me unattractive."

"What? No."

"Oh, so *you* find me attractive?"

His eyes narrowed. "Are you trying to keep me from finding out about why you are crying?"

She sighed. The man always knew what she was up to.

"No. Not really. It's just an emotional day. Your sister is married and pregnant. And I'm leaving Tuesday."

"Leaving? Where are you going?" he demanded.

She was taken back for a moment. Aeden was acting almost angry at her.

"Uh, Africa. I'm going to work with a charity there for six months."

"Why didn't you tell me?"

Once again she hesitated as she tried to process his question and his tone. "Tell you?"

"I meant the family. My family. Why didn't you tell them?"

"I just found out. I'm taking over someone's position since she has to come back early."

His frown turned darker. "I don't think you should go."

"Excuse me?"

"You heard me."

She did. Hard not to since Aeden was always so damned loud and they were in a very small space together.

"Well, I am going to do it. And really, where do you get off telling me if I should or should not do this?"

For a long moment, he said nothing. Wendy studied him, her gaze raking over him, taking one last look at him. He had always been pretty as all the Fitzpatricks. Blond hair, blue eyes, and a core sense of goodness they all seemed to have. The longer the moment drew out, the harder her heart beat.

"So, you have no answer?"

He muttered something under his breath then he grabbed her and yanked her against him. Before she could think, he crushed his mouth down on hers.

She couldn't think, didn't want to. For years, she'd wondered what it would be like to kiss him, to feeling those strong arms wrapped around her body as he teased her with that glorious mouth of his. Now, she knew, and she was damned well going to take advantage of it.

Wendy slipped her hands up over his shoulders then behind his neck as she opened her mouth to his teasing tongue. She didn't realize he had backed her against the wall until she felt it against her back. As he pressed closer, she felt the long length of his erection against her stomach. A shudder of need coursed through her, and she shivered. She was far from being a virgin, but nothing had prepared her for Aeden. As his hands roamed over her body, she forgot where they were, what was going on, and even who they had been before this. All that filled her mind was how he made her feel.

Aeden broke away from her but kept her in his arms. "Well...we don't seem to have much self-control."

She chuckled and tried to move, but it caused her breasts to brush against his chest. They both sucked in a breath at the contact. Instead of moving away like she thought he would, leaned closer.

"What are we going to do about this?" he asked, as his breath feathered over her ear.

"What can we do? I'm leaving Tuesday."

He took her earlobe between his teeth and gave it a gentle tug. Then he licked it. She shivered.

"We have tonight."

"Is that the best you can do, Fitzpatrick?" she asked, trying to sound as sarcastic as possible, but her voice trembled, ruining the effect.

He pulled back and looked her straight in the eye. "It's hard to come up with anything better."

"Why is that?"

"You melted my brain, woman."

His gaze didn't waver, and there was no mistaking the truth laid bare for her. It wasn't something she would expect from Aeden. She opened her mouth to answer him, but there was a shout from the main room of the restaurant.

"Things are getting rowdy, and it's only a matter of time before we're discovered," she said.

"Say you'll meet me later."

It wasn't a demand, but a plea. Normally, she would steer clear. Aeden was a complicated man with the problem of Kaitlin being her best friend. Add in the fact that her feelings for him scared the living bejesus out of her, and he was someone Wendy would avoid. She didn't like complications with men, in her professional or personal life. But tonight, he was standing there, and she was leaving in a few days. Dammit, she wanted this...needed it on some primal level.

"Okay. My apartment."

A look of relief passed over his face. Then he gave her a long, hard kiss before stepped back.

"You go on. I'll catch up," he said. She hesitated, and he smiled. "Won't look good if we both walk out there. You know they'll catch on. Besides, I need a moment," he said glancing down.

For the first time in a long time, she blushed, and he chuckled. "You're blushing."

"I am not."

"You are, and it's cute. Go before I haul you into the bathroom."

"Okay," she said and hurried off. It might be a mistake, but it was one she wanted to make. For once, she would throw caution to the wind and indulge herself.

One Night with a Santini

I was searching for something I didn't know what I was missing in my life.

A stopover to New Orleans, I run into my college crush Kaitlin Fitzpatrick and after one night together, I know I want more. Lucky me, I'm moving to her hometown of Baltimore.

Only, by the time I arrive, she's got news neither of us were expecting.

She's not sure about us, and this added complication doesn't mean we will get our happily ever after. Worse, she has an annoying family of brothers who want to protect her from me.

Thankfully, I was raised a Santini and we have happily ever after tattooed across our hearts.

Brando Santini sidestepped a rather inebriated man as he walked down the corridor of his New Orleans hotel. There was something to be said for staying right on Bourbon Street, and not all of it good. The hotel was impeccable, and with the easy access to the most famous street in the United States, he and his buddies didn't have to worry about a designated driver. Still, no matter how good the clientele was, New Orleans brought out the worst in a lot of people. Expensive rooms and a world-class staff didn't keep people from overindulging.

He hit the button for the elevator and stepped back. He tried to ignore the fact that the man he'd passed was now vomiting in a trashcan. Brando didn't have a weak stomach, but when he could smell soured liquor wafting down the hallway, he had to swallow a couple of times. Finally, he heard the man stumble off. Brando didn't think he had ever gotten that drunk in his life. He might like a buzz every now and then, but losing complete control was not something he wanted to do.

His cell rang and he knew it was his twin brother calling to check up on him.

"Hey, Carlos. How's Arizona?" he asked.

"Hot," Carlos said in his regular deadpanned voice. His mother had always said they were a great comedy team. Brando would crack the jokes and Carlos was the straight man.

"But it's a dry heat," Brando said as the elevator doors opened. "I mean, how many times did we hear that about Arizona before?"

"Yeah, right. I guess you would know since you are in the middle of wet hell."

While they were twins, they had different tastes in climate. Brando liked to experience different climates from one day to the next; Carlos was more of the stay in one place kind of guy. They might both be military brats, but Carlos said that he'd had enough travel during their childhood and his former career in the Marines. He was ready to settle down.

Brando waited for a couple people to get off the elevator. "You should have come out here with me."

"I don't like New Orleans. It's hot and noisy. You know how I feel about that."

He didn't have to explain himself to Brando. Since his injury while he was serving in Iraq, Carlos did not like big crowds. He had never been one who liked to party much even before that. Neither of them werc.

"Still, I figured we would spend some time together before I head out east."

"What made you take that job to begin with? With all of us out west, I thought you would want to be out here."

He shrugged, then realized his brother could not see him. "I just wanted to try it out."

Truth was, he had been thinking about it for a couple of years. Teaching ROTC didn't always help an officer's career, but Brando was thinking about AM—After the Marines. Teaching was something he'd wanted to try for a long time. This would at least let him know if he was cut out for the job before he went back to school for a doctorate.

"Okay. Are you stopping by here on your road trip?"

"Yeah, I figured you might be sad and lonely without me."

Carlos laughed. "Yeah, sure. It's just me and my horses. Don't get too drunk, Marine."

"You got it."

The moment he clicked his phone off, it dinged again, telling him that someone in his family had sent him a text. The doors opened as he tapped on the message. He wasn't watching where he was going, and ran into something very soft and curvy. The scent of roses filled his senses.

"Ooph," he said.

When he finally untangled himself, he offered the person he had practically plowed down a smile. In that split second, he was held dumbfounded. Brando blinked...then blinked again. He knew her. He would recognize those amazing blue eyes anywhere.

"Kaitlin Fitzpatrick?"

She shook her head as she focused on his face.

"Brando?" she asked, her voice breathless enough to send his heart skipping a beat or two.

Before she could say anything else, he pulled her into his arms for a hug. All those wondrous curves pressed up against him.

"I can't believe I literally ran into you."

When he released her, her face had turned an adorable shade of pink. Her blonde hair was up in a sassy pony tail. A dangle of silver hoops hung from her ears and the dress. God, the woman was wearing a red sundress that hugged her hips and gave him a hint at cleavage.

When he made eye contact with her again, his brain froze. It was always like this. His ability to talk seemed to dissolve around Kaitlin on a regular basis. From the moment he had met her their freshman year at the University of Maryland, he couldn't seem to form a coherent thought when he looked into her eyes. He could still remember the way he had fantasized about her. He knew that every time he met a woman, he compared her to Kaitlin. And he hadn't even kissed her.

He cleared his throat and brought his mind back to the present.

"How long has it been?" he asked.

She shook her head. "Since graduation. What are you doing

here?" Her gaze roamed over his unruly curls and she frowned. "Did you get out of the Marines?"

He shook his head. "I've been on leave, so I let it grow out a bit."

She laughed and pressed her hand against his jaw. She snapped it back as if she realized she was acting too familiar for a married woman.

"That explains the beard."

He nodded. "I always let it go when I have a week or so off. I'm PCSing out to the East coast."

"Wow, Quantico?"

He laughed. "No. I'm actually going to be in your neck of the woods. Going to be teaching ROTC at Maryland."

Her eyes widened then she chuckled. "I never thought you would end up back there."

"Once a Terrapin always a Terrapin."

"Ain't that the truth."

Then silence. They always had these awkward pauses in their conversation. Most of the problem had been Brando. He was always trying to come up with something else to say to her. He did everything he could to spend more time in her presence.

"So, what happened with you? Did you move back to Baltimore?"

She shook her head. "I stayed in College Park to finish up my Masters' in speech pathology."

"Ah," he said. "And, did you and what's his name get married?"

He could have found out easily enough. They were both on social media and had several friends in common, but Brando had avoided it. He hadn't friended or followed her on any of them. If he didn't hear she was married, he didn't have to deal with the feelings.

Her eyes danced. "His name was Glen and no. We did not get married."

He glanced down at her hand then back at her face. No ring. "Oh?"

"Yeah."

"So, you're not married now?"

She shook her head. "You?"

He shrugged. "I've been deployed a lot. Makes it hard."

And none of them had been Kaitlin. She had become the standard to which he judged every woman.

"I can understand that."

Then a beat of silence filled the air between them again. It had been ten years since he had seen her, and he still felt that tickle in the back of his throat. Hell, his palms were sweaty.

She didn't look that different. Well, a little bit, but for the better. Thank God she was still curvy. He never liked skinny women. He liked his women to have flesh he could hold on to.

"So, you are going out with your brothers tonight?"

He shook his head. "Here with some friends."

She opened her mouth to say something else, when they were interrupted by one of those friends.

"Brando," Chet yelled down the hallway of the hotel.

Several people turned their heads in the direction of Chet. The man had been born on a horse farm in Texas and was as loud as the day was long. He also had the manners of a goat.

Chet made his way through the milling people to reach them. Before reaching them, Chet's gaze focused on Kaitlin. His eyes narrowed, and softened as he smiled. Damn. He recognized the interest in his friend's eyes. Chet was known for his way with women.

"Hey, Brand. Who have we got here?"

His accent had deepened and Brando knew he did it on purpose. It was a tactic Chet used all the time to pick up women. Brando was still surprised that women fell for it.

"Brand?"

Irritation slipped under Brando's skin. "*We* don't have anyone here. She's mine."

Chet's eyebrows rose in surprise and his mouth curved. Thankfully, he didn't say anything. It didn't mean he wouldn't hear about it later.

"I mean, this is Kaitlin Fitzpatrick, an old college friend."

"Nice to meet you, Kaitlin," Chet said.

"Hi," she said.

"So, are you going out with us tonight?" he asked.

"I…" she looked at Brando.

"No. She is not. Go away. I'll catch up with you in a few minutes."

"How will you know where we are?" Chet asked with a knowing grin curving his lips.

"You're going to Bourbon Street. I'll find you."

He nodded. "Oh. Okay. Nice to meet you, Kaitlin."

Chet gave them one long glance before he joined the others at the entrance of the hotel. Brando shoved his hands into his jean pockets to keep from touching her.

"So, are you here for fun?" he asked.

She rolled her eyes. "No. I'm here for a convention. Or have been. I leave tomorrow morning."

Of course. It was his luck with his dream girl. Every time

they seemed to have a chance to get together, something came up. And there had been the pesky problem of the fiancé. At least that loser was gone now.

"Damn." He looked down the hallway where Chet had just disappeared. It was his first night in New Orleans, and he had been ready to party with his friends. Sort of. Now, though, this was more important. "Have you eaten dinner?"

She shook her head. "I was thinking about ordering in. I don't do that very often, but I have had enough of New Orleans for the day."

"Have dinner with me?" he asked before he could help himself. He wanted any and all the time he could get with her.

She opened her mouth, and he was worried she was going to say no. His fate hung in the balance. He didn't know exactly why he was thinking that, but for some reason, him having dinner with Kaitlin seemed vitally important. Like a matter of life and death important. He had one night and knowing she was unmarried, possibly available, was a little bit more than he could ignore.

"Okay. That sounds wonderful, in fact."

He let loose the breath he had been holding and smiled. "Great. Have any place in mind? This is my first night in New Orleans."

"Oh." She glanced down the hallway where Chet had walked, then back to him. "Are you sure you want to eat dinner with me then?"

He smiled. "I can assure you that there is one thing I want to do tonight, and that is spend time with you. How about the little restaurant across the street?"

"I haven't been there, but a couple people said it was good."

"Great." He held out his arm. "Ready?"

She looked down at his arm, then back at him. The shy smile that curved her lips tugged at his heart and did more amazing things to the rest of his body.

"Let's go."

About the Author

From an early age, USA Today Best-selling author Melissa loved to read. When she discovered the romance genre, she started to listen to the voices in her head. After years of following her AF Major husband around, she is happy to be settled in Northern Virginia surrounded by horses, wineries, and many, many Wegmans.

Keep up with Mel, her releases, and her appearances by subscribing to her <u>NEWSLETTER</u>. If you want to keep up with cover reveals, new behind the scene info on her writing, and when new excerpts are posted, follow her MelissaSchroeder.net News News. Or you can do both! They are low traffic, so you will not get tons of emails.

Check out all her other books, family trees and other info at <u>her website!</u>
<u>If you would want contact Mel, email her at: melissa@ melissaschroeder.net</u>

instagram.com/melschro

amazon.com/author/melissa_schroeder

facebook.com/MelissaSchroederfanpage

bookbub.com/authors/melissa-schroeder

goodreads.com/Melissa_Schroeder

tiktok.com/@melissawritesromance